A Time of Fire

Robert Westall was born in 1929 on Tyneside, where he grew up during the Second World War. He studied Fine Art at Durham University, and Sculpture at the Slade in London, before teaching art in schools in the North of England. He was also a branch director of the Samaritans, a journalist and an antique dealer. Between 1985 and his death in 1993, he retired to devote himself to his writing.

His first novel for children, *The Machine Gunners*, published by Macmillan in 1975, won the Carnegie Medal. He won it again in 1982 for *The Scarecrows* (the first writer to win the medal twice), the Smarties Prize in 1989 for *Blitzcat*, and the Guardian Award in 1991 for *The Kingdom by the Sea*.

Reviews of Robert Westall's work:

'A writer who managed to combine literary excellence with an immense talent for capturing the imagination and interest of child and, in particular, young adult readers.'
Independent

'Westall was a writer of rare talent. We shall miss him, but he has left us such a wonderful legacy.'
Michael Morpurgo, *Guardian*

Books by Robert Westall

A Time of Fire

Robert Westall

MACMILLAN CHILDREN'S BOOKS

First published 1994 by Macmillan Children's Books

This edition published 2002 by Macmillan Children's Books
a division of Macmillan Publishers Limited
20 New Wharf Road, London N1 9RR
Basingstoke and Oxford
www.panmacmillan.com

Associated companies throughout the world

ISBN 0 330 39864 4

3 5 7 9 8 6 4 2

A CIP catalogue record for this book is available from
the British Library

Typeset by Intype London Ltd
Printed and bound in Great Britain by Mackays of Chatham plc, Kent

For Mary Tapissier
Memories of Baika

1

Sonny walked home whistling. Life was good in spite of the War.

Not that there'd been much War so far in Newcastle. The siren had gone twice during lessons, sending them scurrying down the new school shelter like well-disciplined lines of black beetles, gas masks thumping against backsides. There, they'd sung patriotic songs like 'There'll Always be an England'. And whistled like soldiers when the lights suddenly went out, which they always did. In the exciting dark they had stamped their feet in the puddles on the concrete floor, sending water splashing up the girls' knickers and making them scream. Then the all-clear had gone and they had filed blinking up into the daylight again, to find the world disappointingly unchanged. It had only been solitary Jerry bombers photographing the ships in the river, the paper said afterwards.

There had been a gas mask practice, when they had to file through a room full of tear gas, and Charlie Blower's gas mask had leaked and he sat in the classroom for half an hour tears streaming down his face, though he had assured everybody he felt quite cheerful, just blind. Then he'd been sent home for the rest of the day, lucky swine.

They had hunted for signs of the War feverishly.

Some of the ships moored in the river now had big guns on their sterns, though sadly these were hidden by tarpaulins. Harry Hardy reckoned this was to baffle the Nazi spies, but everyone else reckoned it was just to keep the rain off. Once word had come there was a real destroyer moored at the Quay, with four 4.7-inch guns and eight torpedo tubes. Sonny had run all the way to see it, but when he got there there was no smoke coming out of its single funnel, so he needn't have hurried and made himself feel sick. But the four gun-turrets and the gleaming range-finder were so real and marvellous that he'd felt quite sick all over again.

But since that wonderful day, nothing had happened really. The War was a bore. At the start, half the lads in his class had cancelled their comics and bought *War Weekly* instead. And then swopped halfway through the week with the lads who bought *War Illustrated*. They had hung huge maps of Europe on their bedroom walls, and stuck in little British and Swastika flags on pins. But the pins never moved, and the *War Weekly* was only full of gallant British Tommies in France, giving the thumbs-up from their bren-gun carriers, so Sonny had cancelled *War Weekly* and gone back to the *Wizard*.

Other things were more important than the War now. It was nearly Christmas, and he had brought home his school report, the best ever, especially in maths and handiwork. Dad, fresh from Armstrong Siddeley's and still black in the face, had grinned and said, 'We'll make an engineer of you yet,' which was the highest possible praise. And at the weekend he had had his reward, a trip to the wondrous toyshop,

Alfred and Warner's in the Haymarket, to choose his Christmas present. He would have liked lots of model tanks and guns, but Dad had set his heart on a great steam-boiler and engine, all glistening brass and chrome. Watching Dad's clever engineer's fingers playing with the connecting-rods and dials, Sonny had resigned himself to having guns and tanks for his next birthday instead. Mam had objected that the boiler was German-made, Marklin. But Dad had said the Germans were good engineers, not rubbish like the Japs, and bought it anyway.

But, even more important, tonight was Monday, the night the *Wizard* came into the newsagent's, and he'd called and got it, not willing to wait till the morning. And he'd peeped and there were extra-long stories about his two heroes: the great Wilson, who ran the three-minute mile in the Berlin Olympics at the age of a hundred, because he lived on a diet of special herbs given him by a mysterious hermit on the Yorkshire Moors. And the Wolf of Kabul, still outwitting Nazi agents on the North-west Frontier and Afghanistan. Even Wilson was working for the War Effort now, doing a lot more than the useless Tommies in their bren-gun carriers in France . . .

Still whistling, Sonny turned in at his gate, past the useless air-raid shelter that was half-full of water that Dad used for the chrysanths in his greenhouse. He reached for the door-key, hung on a string inside the letter-box, dumped his bag, and was instantly alongside the Wolf of Kabul.

Twenty minutes later he was still leaning on the kitchen window sill, straining to read by the last of the daylight. He knew it was getting late; outside the sky was a dark, clear blue, against which the barrage balloons, still in sunlight, glinted their silver sides like stars. They were high tonight, whatever that meant . . .

He was half-frozen, even inside his school mac. He knew he should have put a match to the kitchen fire, all laid ready by Mam with sticks and paper. He knew he should draw the blackout curtains and put the light on so he didn't ruin his eyes. But in far Afghanistan, the Wolf of Kabul was *really* in trouble, bound hand and foot in a police cell, with the firing-squad gathering outside.

And then the garden gate clicked, and he looked through the window to see Mam coming up the path, a laden leather shopping bag in each hand. He waited till she vanished inside the porch, then swiftly drew the blackout curtains, flick, flick, made sure there was no chink of daylight showing, and put the light on. He scurried around looking for a box of matches to light the fire, but couldn't find one. And then she was in the kitchen with him, putting the bags on the table with a puff of relief.

'By, that hill gets steeper, but Aah get no younger.' Then she saw the unlit fire. 'Oh, Sonny, this kitchen's perishing. Your poor Dad, gettin in freezin' from work . . .'

'I couldn't find any matches, Mam!'

'Aah *told* you this morning! Get some from the paper shop when you get your comic! Aah *gave* you the tuppence! Aah put it in your coat pocket . . .'

Too late he remembered, groped in his pocket. The tuppence for the Swan Vestas was still there.

With Dad there would have been a row. But Mam just shook her head and raised her eyebrows in incredulous disbelief. Then smiled at him as if he was the most precious thing in the world.

'Eeh, you're a proper dreamboat. Chock-full of your weird ideas. You'd forget your head if it was loose. Give us the tuppence. Aah'll go meself.'

'No, Mam, I'll go, I'll go!' He was full of repentance.

'No, Aah want them tonight, not tomorrow. You stay an' finish your old comic. Wolf of Kabul in trouble again, is he?'

He saw her so clearly, little and plump and smiling at him, with her rosy cheeks and oldest headscarf round her head for shopping. Then she turned and walked out. Sonny could tell from her walk that she was weary, and that made him feel even guiltier.

But the *Wizard* still drew him. The Wolf of Kabul's servant had shown up in the nick of time, and cracked open several Nazi and Afghan skulls with his famous weapon, the cricket bat he called 'Clicky-ba'. Things were looking up.

And then Sonny heard the sound of a plane's engines. He would have run out anyway. Planes were an even bigger draw than the Wolf. Planes to quarrel about at school, over the aircraft-recognition charts they all carried in their pockets. Blenheims and Defiants, Heinkels and Dornier Flying Pencils . . .

But this plane was coming in low and unbelievably fast. Once in the garden on top of the air-raid shelter, the sound began to deafen him. *Never* a plane this low! Even in the dusk, he would see every detail of it, the cockpit, the guns . . .

He held his hands over his ears to protect them. He felt the plane was going to land on top of him. But still his eyes searched the sky eagerly.

They came and went in the time he took to blink. Not one plane but two. All that was left on his eyes after was two giant superimposed black shapes, the first with two engines, the second with one. And from the second, bright flashes.

And then the sky split open. A sky all of brilliant yellow light; a world of noise that filled his ears like sand at the seaside, so that afterwards there was only total silence. Something picked him up and threw him off the shelter top into the privet hedge, where he hung until a great wind came the other way and threw him flat on his back.

He staggered to his feet, winded, clawing for breath. He could hear nothing, he could see nothing. Terror filled him until he saw, very dimly, a black telegraph pole silhouetted against the dusky sky. So he was not blind. He shoved fingers in his ears to try to prove he was not deaf.

The first sound he heard, very faintly, was the air-raid siren going. He knew he should take cover, but he was too busy getting his breath back, and proving by looking and listening to everything that he was not blind or deaf.

Then an air-raid warden grabbing him, shouting, 'Get down the shelter,' and almost pushing him down into the water Dad used for his chrysanths. He struggled, pointing out the water.

'Get indoors then. Get indoors, son! Under the stairs is safest.'

The man thrust him indoors and under the stairs, which was full of the gas-meter and sacks of potatoes Dad had laid in against the winter. The odd faint whiff of gas came to him, and the smells of soil and sacking, which were a comfort.

But scarcely had he settled than the all-clear went, the long straight note. He rushed out, all eagerness to tell the first person he met how he'd been deaf and blind and couldn't breathe but now he was marvellously all right again.

He headed towards the next street where the news-agent's was, because the person he really wanted to tell most was Mam. And because in this direction there were exciting signs of damage. Slates off the roofs, showing the dark rafters. Windows blown out, with torn, ghostly curtains drifting like phantom hands through the broken glass. He began to meet people all wandering in the same direction, calling to each other to know where the bomb had dropped. But no one could say, because no one knew anything, except it had been close.

And then they turned the corner, into the next street, and no one had to ask or tell.

The street was littered with bricks.

And, like an extracted tooth, alone of all the houses, the newsagent's shop was gone.

He ran to join the ring of people gathering; his heart nearly stopped beating with the most dreadful fear. Everywhere he looked for Mam's face. And did not see it. Every other face he knew, Mrs Fogarty, Mrs Belmont, old Granny Cash . . .

Then old Granny Cash saw him, and her face, with all the wrinkles of her years of hardship, formed into a far more dreadful face of pain than he had ever seen.

'For God's sake get that little bairn out of here!' she cried.

And then he knew that Mam had been inside the shop.

2

It seemed to Sonny, when he awakened with a jump next morning, that he was in a burrow like a rabbit. The whole house was inside the burrow, and Dad and Nana and Granda were inside with him. And the rest of the world outside had really ceased to exist. It all belonged to yesterday, when Mam was alive; it was a place he was shut off from for ever.

He looked out at this lost world through his window. Tommy Foster, who was his best mate at school and at home, was coming down the road. Tommy belonged to the lost world as well. Sonny could no more have opened the window and shouted to him than he could have flown to the moon.

But, as he watched in a dreary, bored way, it seemed to Sonny that Tommy had problems as well. Tommy got to within twenty yards, and then looked up fearfully at Sonny's house. Almost as if some monster lived there, like Dracula or Frankenstein. Then Tommy crossed the road to the far pavement, and scuttled past with nervous looks, as if in terror of his life.

Then Sonny realized that he was the monster Tommy was afraid of. Mam had died, and turned the whole family into monsters. In the demolished newsagent's Mam alone had died; that was the unbelievable thing. The newsagent had nipped out for five minutes, to deliver a paper that some silly paper lad had forgotten to take in his sack. The newsagent's wife, suddenly taken short in the shop, had excused herself to Mam, and left her waiting there while she slipped down to the outdoor privy at the bottom of her yard. She had been dug out of a mountain of bricks with no more than bruises. The newsagent's children had been to their gran's for tea. And all the other bombs had landed behind the newsagent's shop, on some allotments, where they had killed one lop-eared rabbit.

One lop-eared rabbit. And Mam.

Sonny watched Tommy till he vanished round the far corner. He would never get to speak to Tommy again. People didn't speak to monsters. But, when the whole world was pressing down on you, a little thing like Tommy Foster scarcely mattered . . .

Sonny had killed Mam. If he hadn't forgotten the matches, she would be in the kitchen now, bustling about, washing up after breakfast. And if he had gone for the matches, instead of Mam, he would be dead instead.

The two facts made him feel strange beyond belief. So strange he almost felt outside his body. Observing his body breathing, moving, drinking, even speaking, just as usual. Only he wasn't speaking more than he had to, because every time he opened his mouth he was afraid his dreadful secret might fly out, and then not even Nana or Granda or Dad would ever speak to him again . . . and that would be the end of him. Again, he wished that he'd gone for the matches himself . . .

'Ah, you're awake!' said Nana, bustling in, making

him jump. 'Your breakfast's ready. Aah've done your favourite, fried bread wi' an egg fried both sides.'

'I'm not hungry,' said Sonny. And indeed *something* was neatly filling up his inside, right to the back of his throat. He did not feel sick, just full to the brim, as if he'd just eaten a large, bitter heavy pudding.

'Oh, we cannit have that,' said Nana. 'Your poor Dad's got enough on his plate, wi'out worrying about you not eating. He didn't feel like eatin' either, nor your Granda. But they got it down them. You've got to keep up your strength. C'mon, just a little bit, to please me. Aah cooked it special for you.'

Sonny looked at her. The rims of her eyes were very red. Somewhere, sometime, she had cried a lot. But now her lips were set in their usual determined way, and her massive folded arms looked ready to do anything that needed doing. It came to him that she was going to . . . go on. Survive. That was the word. Nobody was asking him to live, or laugh, or play, or do lessons. All of which were quite impossible now. He was being asked merely to survive. And that he thought he could just about manage.

The next day, Nana gently coaxed him into going for a little walk, to get a bit of fresh air. At first, he was glad to get out of the house, for the winter sun was shining, and all the other houses and gardens looked the same as ever, and he had an odd burst of happiness that almost convinced him that it was all a bad dream, and that nothing had happened at all. But then he saw Mrs Brown their next-door neighbour coming down the street towards him and he grew terribly afraid, and ran across the road and

11

ducked down an alley. After that he wandered with his head down, close to the wall, hunched up as if fearing a blow. So he never saw the looks people gave him; the way they crossed the street to avoid meeting him. He was just puzzled he met nobody else he knew; but glad of it.

The place he avoided most of all, apart from the gaping hole where the newsagent's had been, was the church. For God lurked inside the church, and God knew about the matches. God was lurking inside the church like a tiger, waiting to pounce . . .

It was therefore with utter horror that Sonny came out of his daze at last, and realized the church was between him and home. To avoid it would mean a half-mile extra, and now Sonny's legs were so weary he could hardly put one in front of the other.

He crept past on the opposite side of the road. He was *almost* past when a voice he knew said, 'Hello, Sonny!' A rich, posh voice.

His eyes crept outwards from his feet. Took in the cracked, shiny, black shoes with their silver buckles, the tall column of black cloth above, the scuffed broad leather belt with the little crucifix hanging from it, and, last, the pudgy bespectacled face of Father Pestle, with his mop of curly black hair. To Sonny's nostrils came that dreadful scent of holiness; incense and candlewax, dust and hymn books. God had struck. He was in the jaws of the beast. He would be torn apart. His short life was over.

He tried a last desperate plea for life; he tried to plead 'Let me go!' But his throat would not work. His mouth opened and shut and nothing came out but a meaningless croak, as he stared at the black

12

buttons of Father Pestle's cassock that ran all the way up from his feet to his neck.

He would never know how Father Pestle was tempted to despair: to turn away from the small hopeless bundle of misery in front of him, to whom nothing could possibly be said that would mean anything. He would never know how Father Pestle thought of his own mother, alive and well, and was ashamed. How Father Pestle realized that if his own mother had died, he would not have been able to go on at all. He would never know how tempted Father Pestle was to smile at him and ruffle his hair affectionately and flee into the safety of his own vestry . . .

But Father Pestle steeled himself and played the man. He took Sonny gently by one shoulder and said kindly,

'Let's go into church for a minute.' Though he trembled and prayed desperately for a strength and clear sight he knew he did not have.

To Sonny, his hand was a policeman's hand. More, the hand of God himself. Like a condemned murderer, he let himself be led to trial and execution. It was a relief, really. How had he ever thought he could get away with it? God knew every step he took . . .

They were in the church now; in the dark. Only the huge, pointed, blue windows gave a dim light, and within that light, the walls of Jericho fell and tumbled for ever, and God turned Lot's wife to a pillar of salt, and the saints and prophets turned their terrible bearded faces to look at Sonny as he passed. And, even dimmer in the darkness, the life-size angels glimmered their white robes and gold wings and cold uncaring faces. The whole court of Heaven was

13

assembled for the trial, and now he was led to the feet of the Judge, the awful judge who hung in agony on the Cross, the blood oozing from his gaping wounds in round, red blobs.

Father Pestle sat with a leathery creak, and forced Sonny down beside him. Sonny's one thought was of Mam. Somewhere, he thought, in the back corridors of Heaven, Mam must be struggling to reach him, defend him. But what was Mam in comparison to the saints and angels? They would never let her through in time; they would not listen to her . . .

But he said, as if with his last breath (for it had become very difficult to breathe):

'Mam!'

'Yes?' said Father Pestle, coaxingly, because he couldn't think of anything else to say. But it was enough. It all came out of Sonny's mouth in a rush, all about the matches. And finally there was silence, and, oddly, Sonny felt a bit better, though not much. Like when he'd had that boil and Dad had squeezed it with steaming cloths and it had finally burst.

But Father Pestle was seized with an almost drunken joy; for he could see a way to help for once, a way to be of use.

'Sonny,' he said, in a stern voice, because there must be no softness, only sternness would work and cure. 'Sonny, you know you must tell the uttermost truth, here at the feet of God?'

Sonny nodded.

'Tell God then. What would have happened that night if the German pilot had not dropped his bombs?'

That threw Sonny into a whirl. It was not at all

the kind of question he had expected God would ask. But the answer came, in jerks, like a train shunting.

'Mam woulda . . . come home . . . with the matches . . . lit the fire . . . got the supper. All just . . . the usual.'

'Good.' Father Pestle made his voice even sterner, though his heart leapt again with joy. 'So God wants to know . . . wants you to tell him, out loud . . . who killed your Mam?'

Sonny took a long time, and there was a deep silence, while God and the saints and prophets and angels, the whole court of Heaven, listened. But he felt something inexorable (which might be God himself) pushing him towards the only possible answer.

'The . . . the . . . Jerry pilot.'

'You have told God the truth,' said Father Pestle. 'That pilot, that dreadful man, that murderer of women . . . he may not know what he has done now, as he flies so high in the air. But God is not mocked, Sonny. That dreadful man will come to his judgement. And if he does not repent, Sonny, and that right soon, he will burn in Hell for it.'

Sonny took a deep shuddering breath. It was as if some huge flaming thing had missed him by a hair's breadth, and swept the unknown pilot screaming to his doom.

'There,' said Father Pestle, gentler now the work was done. 'You have told the truth. God is pleased with you, Sonny. The courts of Heaven rejoice that the truth has been told.'

It was unbelievable. God was no longer after him,

15

like a dreadful tiger. But no sooner had one horror vanished, than another replaced it.

'Me Dad. I haven't told me Dad . . .'

'Shall we go and tell your Dad together?' Father Pestle was almost euphoric now, didn't understand. Sonny looked at him with horror.

'I can't tell me Dad. *He'll* never forgive me. He's not like . . . God.'

Father Pestle bit his lip. He knew Dad and his temper. Dad had walked out of church one Christmas Eve, when he hadn't been asked to take the collection when he reckoned it was his turn. And hadn't come back for a year, in spite of Mam's pleadings.

'Then you must make it up to your Dad in other ways. You are all your Dad has in the world now. You must be a good son to him.' Never argue with him; do as he wants, always try to be what he wants you to be . . .'

'Yes,' said Sonny. 'Yes.'

Father Pestle blessed him then, laying his hands on his head and pressing down so hard that Sonny felt his neck might give way. Then they walked out into the sunlight, somehow hand in hand.

It was only that night, in the middle of his lonely prayers, that something began to trouble Father Pestle. Oh, he was sure it had worked for Sonny.

But the German pilot . . . he was somebody's son too. Probably frightened all the time, perhaps bewildered, if he was any kind of decent man at all . . . Had he *cursed* the German pilot, in his own rage and grief for the child? He knew all pilots were afraid of fire; far more than anything else. That talk of hell-fire . . .

16

Uneasy, he tossed and turned on his narrow bed all night. Perhaps he should talk to the child again. But how, without making the father suspicious? Perhaps if he met the child in the street?

But even Father Pestle in all his wisdom could not begin to fathom what he had started.

3

They got home from the funeral frozen to the bone. But the house soon felt too hot to Sonny, with fires in every room and people everywhere. The lounge was a forest of men in dark suits, holding up the tails of their jackets and warming their bums at the fire. The dining room was full of towers of sandwiches, piles of cakes and biscuits, knives and serviettes, and strange ladies in pinafores and hats bustling to and fro. The kitchen was full of women in black, clustered round the warmth of the range, their faces so pale and lined under their hats that Sonny didn't recognize them until they spoke to him. Few of them addressed him anyway, and those that did spoke in loud unnatural voices, as if they were talking to a pet cat or a foreigner or something. But they all watched him out of the corner of their eyes, and their mutterings fell silent when they saw him near. So he moved restlessly from room to room in a bubble of silence. He wondered if they'd guessed about the matches . . .

He tried to flee upstairs. But there, Mam and Dad's bed was piled with a mountain of dark coats, and his own bed too. And there wasn't even a refuge in the lav, because there were three women waiting to use it.

He so much wanted to be alone; to cry in peace. But there was nowhere, nowhere. Even his beloved Nana was too busy to notice him, as she went up to each new arrival to ask in a low voice whether they wanted whisky or sherry. All the men said whisky and all the women sherry. The men drank their whisky in one big gulp, said, 'By, I needed that,' and asked for another straight away. The women seemed to take one sip of theirs, then put it down on some shelf or window sill and forget it.

Far off, he could hear them talking about his mother in tones of hushed reverence, like she'd been God.

'Isn't there any of *her* family here?'

'Why, no. They all went off to Canada in the 1920s, to make their fortunes. Ma, Da, brothers and sisters. Only Maggie stayed, because she was waiting to marry our Tommy.'

'Aye, she was a good wife, and a grand little mother . . .'

'A grand lass. Salt of the earth . . .'

'A good wife, and a good little mother.'

'Aye, she was a grand little lass. Salt of the earth . . .' Always do anyone a good turn.'

'She was very good to us, when our Henry was born. Couldn't do enough.'

'She'd not have been more than . . . thirty-five?'

'Aye, the good die young!'

'The Lord calls you when he wants you!'

'Well, she's in a better place now!'

Sonny grew confused. Why did they think Heaven was a better place than home? How did they *know*? And if they really thought that, why did they all look as if the end of the world had come? Sweating, pale. Then he heard someone say,

'You wonder who'll be taken next!'

19

That was when Sonny made his great discovery: how afraid the adults were of dying. Which was funny, because he wasn't the least afraid of it himself, now he was OK with God. Mam would be waiting for him, smiling, and he could say he was sorry about the matches, and she would say it didn't matter at all. Then they could go off and see the things in Heaven together.

He came to with a start. Silence had fallen in the lounge, the dining room, the hall. Which left the way clear for a woman sobbing her heart out in the kitchen. But it also left the way clear for Nana, standing unafraid in her hat and pinny, to say, 'There's lots to eat. I want everybody to tuck in, because we don't want anything wasted, not in wartime. You've got to eat, to keep your strength up. I'm sure that's what our Maggie would have wanted. She hated wasting good food.'

Like magic, the mood changed. Everyone became very helpful, passing round plates and serviettes and sandwiches. Now, the talk was of the good old days. It was as if Mam had risen from her coffin in the cold, hard ground, and become not just alive, but a pretty young girl again.

'Aye, she loved to dance. Best dancer Aah ever saw. You remember her in the Charleston?'

'Happy days, lively days. You remember them notices they used to put up in the Assembly Rooms? "Please Charleston quietly", PCQ for short?'

'And at home, in their front room. Roll back the carpet. Out with the old gramophone.'

'And the girls, walking along the Top, arm in arm,

every Saturday night? And all the lads walking the opposite way, making wise-cracks?'

'Aye, she was a quick one wi' her tongue, was Maggie. Never a feller yet got the better of her.'

And then, as the mountains of sandwiches dissolved, like old snow in the sun, and the dirty plates were passed back, and the rattle of washing-up replaced the sobbing from the kitchen, people even began to talk of other things.

'Busy at the Yard, Gordon?'

A total stranger stroked his bald head, and said, 'Busy? Eight till eight, seven days a week. We're worn out.'

'Plenty of overtime money, though?'

'Aye, plenty of money an' no time to spend it. We've got a Norwegian timber-boat in dry dock. Hit by a torpedo off Blyth, but her timber kept her afloat. You should see the hole in her hull. You could drive a double-decker through it.'

And then people were going, fetching hats and coats from upstairs, helping each other on with them. Forming a little queue to shake hands with Dad, who stood by the lounge mantelpiece, face pale and set.

'Take care of yourself now, Tom. We'll be thinking of you. Anything we can do, you know you've only got to ask.'

But they struggled to keep relief and gladness from their voices; glad to be going back to where life would be quite ordinary again.

And every time the front door opened, to let a couple out, the house got a little colder, a little more silent. As if there were vultures of cold and silence outside, clustered on every rooftop and chimney, only

21

waiting for the last person to go so they could flap down in safety and eat the family up.

The front door banged shut for the last time. Nana came in from shutting it, sat down with the ghost of her usual comfortable sigh, closed her eyes and said, That's done, then!'

Dad had gone to the window and was staring at the sunset. It was a magnificent red sunset, as if God was saying goodbye as well. A few dark birds, high up, flew into sight and then flew slowly out of sight again.

Sonny saw that both Nana and Granda, who was sitting wrestling his huge, wrinkly hands between his knees, were staring at Dad's back. The silence was terrible, the waiting in the silence. Sonny just knew some other dreadful thing was going to happen.

Finally Dad said, without turning, 'Aah'm goin' to join the RAF. I'm going to get that beggar who killed her.'

Sonny heard Granda breathe in sharply.

Then Nana said, and she sounded as if her heart was breaking,

'Eeh, you cannit! What about the bairn here? What about this house? What about yer job?'

Dad's voice grew harsher, till it sounded like when he was sharpening the carving-knife on its steel, before he attacked the Sunday joint.

'Aah cannit stay here. Aah'd go bloody bonkers, thinkin' about that beggar up out there somewhere.'

Granda said, sorrowfully, and as if to a little child, 'You'll never see that feller again. He's one of thousands. Hitler's got hundreds o' bombers.'

It was now that the voice of Father Pestle came

back to Sonny. Help your father; help him all you can. And he spoke, his voice cracking oddly in the middle. His other great secret, that he'd kept to himself till now . . .

'Dad, I know what that plane was. It was a Dornier Flying Pencil . . .'

Dad crossed the room in two violent strides; grabbed Sonny by the wrist so hard it was agonizing.

'Yer don't know what yer talking about!' But there was a wild hope in his voice just the same.

'Dad, I do. I saw it. I was out on top of the shelter when it flew over. I saw it. Closer than the bottom of our garden. It was a Flying Pencil. I can show you, in my book.'

Feverishly he got his aircraft-recognition book out of his pocket; even today, in his best suit, it was there. There was magic inside it . . .

'Look, Dad, the Jerries have only got three two-engined bombers. And the Heinkel's fat, with a fat, round tail. And the Junkers 88's got a pointed tail, with round ends. But the Flying Pencil's tail has got square ends, 'cos it's got two tailfins, one on each end.' He went on and on, pointing out the differences. Dad listened as he'd never listened before, running his work-roughened forefinger across the little black shapes. Finally he said, taking Sonny by the shoulders and looking him full in the eyes, from about six inches away,

'Sonny – are you sure?'

Sonny closed his eyes and saw again, indelibly drawn on his memory, the great blurred shape of the bomber. And compared it to the small, sharp, black drawing. They matched exactly.

23

'Yes.'

Dad let him go. 'Out of the mouths of babes and sucklings,' he said to Granda. Then he turned back to Sonny again, as if some new suspicion had been aroused.

'That British fighter that was following the Jerry, Sonny. What was that?'

Sonny took a deep breath; he knew he was under test. But it wasn't at all a hard test. Anyone could tell a Hurricane with its straight wings, from a Spitfire with its curved ones.

'A Hurricane,' he said.

'Aye,' said Dad, nodding. 'I'd heard it was a Hurricane from Usworth. Nowt wrong wi' your eyes.'

Sonny felt so proud, to be able to help Dad. He wanted to help him more. 'The Germans haven't got many Dorniers, Dad. They're old planes and not much good. They mainly have Heinkels and Junkers.'

'Aye,' said Dad. 'The picture's gettin' clearer. It's been a Dornier that's been sneakin' up the river alone, photographing the ships. Well, one day soon, he'll find me waiting for him.'

'Are you going to be a pilot, Dad?' Grand visions of his father in uniform with wings floated in front of Sonny's eyes.

'No, son.' Dad shook his head bitterly. 'Aah haven't got the education to be a pilot. But they're crying out for air gunners. An' they tell me there's a new fighter-plane coming out, wi' room for an air gunner—'

'The Bolton Paul Defiant,' said Sonny, his whole spine tingling with pride. It was such a grand name.

'The Defiant, eh? Well, Defiants it will be. Aah was

24

always a good shot wi' the old air rifle, wasn't I, Father?'

But it was Nana who raised her voice. 'This is barmy. You're all we've got, now Maggie's gone. D'you want this poor bairn to have no father, as well as no mother? Are ye mad? Ye're a foreman-fitter at Armstrong Siddeley's – mekkin' cars for the Army – reserved occupation – good money – a job against the world. And now you want to go an' get yerself killed an' all.' Her eyes brimmed with tears.

'What good's money to me now Maggie's gone? Aah could have a million pounds in me pocket, an' aah wouldn't knaa what to do wi' it.'

'But the bairn – he's your son.'

'Mother, Aah've prayed to God every night to put this Nazi into me hands. An' look what Sonny's given me . . . God is not mocked.'

Looking at Dad, standing so stiffly, hands clenched on the back of a chair, Sonny felt . . . strange. As if Dad was not quite the Dad he'd always known. As if Dad had become some dangerous stranger . . .

Granda stirred in his chair. He said, sadly, 'Leave the lad be, Mother. He has to do what he has to do. Let him go – there's no shame in joining the RAF.'

'But . . . the bairn?'

'The bairn can come to us. It'll be better for him than this place, wi' all the memories. Down Tynemouth, he can make a fresh start. Forget . . . mebbe.'

Dad said, in a small choked voice, from his place against the sunset, 'Thanks, Father.'

'That's all right, son. You do what's best for you.'

'Aah'll go to the recruiting office in the morning. There's nowt to keep me here now.'

'Aye well, that's settled then. You'd best come home with us tonight an' all. I don't want you alone, brooding here.'

Sonny, bewildered, thought his Dad had become like a little boy again, with Granda as the real father. Granda knew what was best. Almost imperceptibly, Sonny moved towards Granda, and sat down on the arm of his chair. Granda reached out a long arm, clad in dark-blue striped Sunday best, and put it round him, and he suddenly felt safe. Little and weak, but very safe.

'Aye well,' said Nana. 'We'd better get crackin'. Time to pack.' She sighed and got up. Sonny could tell she felt a bit better, just because she knew what she had to do next.

4

At last came the morning for Dad to go. He looked lonely, standing on the front doorstep in his second-best raincoat with the collar turned up, and his only trilby hat. He had a little battered attaché case in his hand.

'Got your razor?' asked Nana. 'You don't want the sergeant-major after you . . .'

'They don't have sergeant-majors in the RAF, Mother, they have flight-sergeants.' There was a sharp edge in Dad's voice. He'd explained that three times already.

'You can't expect women to understand such things,' said Granda soothingly. 'They're not interested.'

'Aye well,' said Nana, 'trouble's trouble, whatever name it goes under. Take care, hinny!' She grabbed Dad hard, and gave him a fierce kiss on the cheek. Dad shuffled a bit with embarrassment.

Granda took his son's smaller hand in a fierce grip. 'The moment ye get off-duty at night, son, gan to bed. Then, when they come round looking for some poor sod to peel spuds in the cookhouse, they won't pick on you.'

He released Dad's hand at last.

'Walk with me as far as the two piers, Sonny?'

'I'll carry your case,' said Sonny.

27

They walked. It was a bleak January morning, with patches of old, rotting snow everywhere. The view out over the piers was lost in sea-fret. The fog-horns at the ends of the piers called through it like lost sea-cows.

'Will you be an air gunner straight away, Dad?'

Dad gave a bitter little laugh. 'Oh, no, they'll teach us the important things first, at Blackpool. How to polish our brasses and blanco our belts. How to salute the high and mighty. Left turn, right turn, about turn, on the Promenade till we don't know if we're coming or going. I'll not see a gun for months; except for some old Boer War rifle to toss about.'

Sonny didn't know whether to be glad or sad.

'They told me once I pass me basic training, I can apply for air gunner.'

'Oh.'

'Livin' wi' your Granda, you're more likely to see that Jerry swine than me. They say he's very fond of the river. You keep your eyes open, and write me straight away if you see him, right?'

'Right.'

There was only the sound of footsteps in the mist.

'Maybe he'll get shot down, Dad, before you get at him?'

'Oh, no.' Sonny felt Dad's mind snap shut like a trap. 'Oh, no. Aah pray to God every night. That feller's goin' to burn in Hell, and Aah'm goin' to send him there. God is not mocked . . .'

Sonny said no more. To say anything else would be dangerous.

'You'd better be gettin' back, or you'll be late for school. Be a good lad for yer Nana and Granda and don't give them any aggravation. They're not as young as they used to be, you know.'

Sonny hated him saying that. Nana and Granda had been the same ever since he'd known them. White hair and wrinkly cheeks and Granda had false teeth. But they were as strong as trees.

They shook hands. Dad said, 'Write to me.' But already Sonny knew his mind was far away.

Sonny watched him walking up the pier-approach road, till he vanished into the mist. Then he turned back towards home.

And suddenly, as if the sun had come out, his heart was lighter. Dad was gone, and with him his silent black rages, when he'd sit for hours, and nobody would hardly dare say a word. Gone were the restless pacing and sudden opening of doors to empty rooms for no reason at all, as if he was still looking for Mam. Gone were the trips to the pub every night, when Granda went with him to keep him out of trouble, though Granda didn't drink that much any more. And the shouting matches late at night, when Sonny had been got safe to bed.

There was only the sea-mist and Nana and Granda now, and their house, the Old Coastguard Station. The world was empty and clean, and he needn't worry he was going to blurt out accidentally about the tuppence and the matches.

It seemed terrible to be glad that Dad was gone. But however much he struggled to unthink the thought, it stayed there.

Granda was waiting for him at the door, smoking his first pipe of the day. Behind him, in the porch, he had arranged three sets of muddy wellies, in order.

First Sonny's small ones, then Dad's middle-sized ones, and then his own huge ones. Like soldiers on parade, all neatly in line.

'They'll be handy there, for when we need them,' said Granda. But Sonny knew it was more than that. It was a promise. Or a hope, anyway.

They listened to the nine o'clock news, then Granda switched off the wireless, to save the batteries. There hadn't been much on the news. Patrol activity on the Western Front. German bombers had tried to bomb Scapa Flow and been driven off by RAF fighters. There was to be more rationing.

''Sem old U-boats,' said Nana. 'They nigh starved us to death in 1917. Aah queued four hours for some giblets and when Aah got to the front of the queue, there was none left.'

'Granda?' said Sonny.

'Eeh,' said Granda, 'it's Granda-Granda non-stop these days. What is it now?'

'Well, you know you were a trawler-skipper?'

'Aye.'

'Well, when you joined up in 1914, why didn't you join the Navy?'

'That's what Aah've always wondered,' said Nana. 'He'd a' been a lot better off, polishing the guns in Scapa Flow an' gettin' four square meals a day . . . None o' that mud an' trenches.'

Granda knocked out his pipe thoughtfully. 'Well, Aah'll tell *you* Sonny, though Aah've never told a living soul till now.'

'You can say that again,' said Nana feelingly.

'Haad yer whisht, woman, while I tell the bairn.

Well, it's like this, Sonny. When Aah was a trawler-skipper, Aah was boss, wasn't Aah? Boss o' me own boat. And once ye've been boss, ye cannit get outa the habit. Aah mean, if Aah'd been on some boat in the Navy, and a storm blew up, an' Aah could see the captain wasn't handling things right, Aah mighta taken the law into me own hands. And then Aah woulda been in real trouble. Mutiny. They used to hang fellers for mutiny ye knaa. Still do, mebbe. So Aah thowt it was safer to go in the Army where Aah didn't knaa me arse from me elbow and Aah would keep me mouth shut.'

'Aah find the idea of *ye* keeping your mouth shut very hard to imagine!' said Nana.

'Granda?'

'Aye?'

'Do you still wish you were a trawler-skipper?'

'Aah'm a bit too old for it now. Awake all night, shootin' the nets. But no, Aah'm glad Aah'm not still a trawler-skipper. An' Aah'll tell you why. Cos Aah was a good one, the best. Nobody could find the shoals like me. Aah had money to burn in me pockets. An' all Aah could think to do wi' it was drinkin' an' fightin'. Being cock o' the walk, even if it meant rolling home black an' blue an' spittin' out teeth. Mind you, it was always a fair fight wi' fists, an' no hard feelin's after. Shake hands an' make up and the best of friends again. Aah only crippled a man for life once. He was a Spaniard an' he pulled a knife on me. Aah broke his arm in two places, so he could never pull a knife on any other poor feller. But ye'd never get a Britisher pullin' a knife in a fight. Only dagoes. But Aah was a bad beggar, and a lot o' grief

31

Aah caused yer Nana. That hawser brekkin' me leg was the best thing ever happened to me. Put me on the straight an' narrow. Made me think. Aah got me compensation money, enough to start the ship's chandlers, an' Aah never looked back. The skippers came to me for their stuff. They knew Aah was one of their own an' would never cheat them. An' Aah had the money to buy this place, when they built the new coastguard station. Nobody else wanted it, stuck out here on the river, no gas, no electric, no runnin' water, no proper lav. They were goin' to pull it down, but Aah saved it. A hundred an' fifty pounds it cost me, an' worth every penny.'

'Granda?'

'*Aye*??'

'*Why* were you a bad beggar?'

'It runs in the family. Black pride. Yer Dad's the same. He was a terrible feller for drinkin' and fightin' till yer Mam got her hands on him. She was the apple of his eye, but by Gum she made him toe the line. When he caalled to take her out of an evening, he had to be perfect. Once she sent him back home cos his shoes weren't polished enough for her likin'. But she was a wise little lass. Started as she meant to go on. No more drinkin'. No more fightin'. Aah don't knaa how he'll manage now she's gone. Aah only hope he saves it up for Jerry, an' not his commanding officer, or he'll be in the glasshouse for a year.'

'Granda?'

'Aye?' Granda looked longingly at the evening paper, which was folded on his chair-arm, half-read. 'Will *I* be a bad beggar?'

Granda cackled. 'That'd be telling . . .'

'Don't torment the bairn,' said Nana, a bit cross.

'Sonny, Aah divven't knaa. Ye've got a lot o' yer Mam in yer. Ye look like her, a lot. But when the time comes . . . ye'll knaa soon enough. Aah expect ye're a chip off the old block . . .'

Sonny was quite pleased. He quite liked the idea of having a bad beggar somewhere inside him, of being a chip off the old block.

'Granda . . . ?'

'Bed!' said Nana firmly. 'Give your Granda a bit o' peace. You can twist him round your little finger.'

Sonny went, reluctantly. As he went, he heard Nana say,

'Why did you never tell me that about the Army?'

'That's fellers' business,' said Granda, and rustled his paper.

Sonny lounged against the rail of the lookout tower where he had his bedroom. It was the kind of February evening that made you think it was spring, even though the grass was brown and dead, and the trees still bare. The setting sun shone on the mouth of the Tyne, enfolded between the arms of the two great piers that stretched a mile out to sea. On his left, every detail picked out in brilliant gold, was the great cliff of Pen-bal-Crag, with the castle where the Army still stood on guard, and the ruins of the Priory, and the flat, grey, concrete shape of the new coastguard station, and the tall radio-masts, and finally the great guns that guarded the harbour.

On his right, across the river, the oil-tanks at South Shields showed their glinting rounded tops through the mist. Behind him, upriver, the ships were moored three abreast with the tall cranes pecking over them like thin, metal herons. The sound of the riveters came chattering faintly across the smooth water; through the mist, showers of sparks from the acetylene welders. The Tyne was working full out, night and day, for the War Effort.

He peered down. Beneath him, two storeys below, the shallow slate roof of Granda's house, and the walls painted white as a seamark for ships entering the river. And all around, looking like a patchwork quilt, Granda's half-acre of garden, inside the low, white garden wall. Not much in it, this time of year. Some rows of ragged and darkening Brussels sprouts, near their end. The pruned berry-bushes, mere stumps. Patches where Granda had turned the soil over, and left the frost to break it up.

He supposed he'd settled in. School was OK. Not that he was really interested, but he did enough to keep out of trouble, keep in the top half of the class. No point to being jeered at as a dummy. He sat next to a boy called Jackie Robinson, a thin lad with big ears and an endless friendly grin that showed everyone he was quite harmless. Sonny had been tackled by the class bully, Podger Armstrong, on his first day. Armstrong, sniffing for trouble, weakness . . .

'Where you from, kid?'

'Newcastle.'

'Wotcher doin' here?'

'Living with me Granda. Me Dad's in the RAF. Training to be an air gunner.'

That didn't do him any harm, with the hovering, waiting, listening group of Armstrong's followers.

34

'Who's your Granda?'

'George Prudhoe.'

That didn't do him any harm with Podger Armstrong either. Granda must have *quite* a reputation . . . Podger raised his eyebrows slightly, and began to lose interest.

'Your Dad send you any machine gun bullets yet?'

'Not yet. He's still square-bashing at Blackpool.'

'When he does, I'll swop you for one. Five glass-alleys, right?'

'Right.' It was a small price to pay for peace. Podger drifted away and began to pick on some much smaller boy.

Jackie Robinson came drifting back, looking relieved. 'You want to watch him. He's a bad beggar . . .'

'Mebbe I'm a bad beggar too,' Sonny had said, grateful to Granda.

Now, he smiled to himself, and took out Dad's last letter.

'Well, Sonny, here we are again. They've given me a corporal's stripes. Local, acting, unpaid of course. I just have to march the squad around, and make sure they keep the barracks spotless. A cross between a nanny and a housewife. The CO said the young lads would take notice of me, being an older man. It's just so the drill-instructors can have a little lie-in in the mornings and sit on their fat backsides. I don't like this CO. He's a sneaky beggar and he's got a file on me. All about me being a foreman at Armstrong Siddeley's and an* *engine-fitter. He started coming it, but I told him straight I'd joined up to be an air gunner, not get my hands dirty with engines. He just gave me his little smirk.*

Hope you are being a good lad and doing well at school and not getting on Nana and Granda's nerves.

Your loving Dad.'

Sonny folded up the letter and put it back in his shirt pocket, inside his jumper and jacket. It was falling apart down the folds, and all fingerprints. Dad didn't write very often . . .

There was a fuss breaking out upriver. Tugboats yipping impudently, and bigger ships answering in long deep notes, like strict schoolmasters. It was time for the convoy to move out, on the evening tide. An armed trawler backed out from the clutter of fishing boats at the Fish Quay half a mile away, her screw thrashing the water into glinting foam. She turned, and came towards him. She looked quite good, even though she wasn't a real warship. Painted all grey, with the rounded, humped foredeck of an Iceland boat; and big, as all the Iceland boats were. Three-inch gun on her foredeck, twin Lewis-guns each side of her bridge, and the cylinders of depth-charges lying in their racks astern. She passed close, while Sonny gloated over all the things that would kill Nazis. She would be a match for a U-boat; on the surface anyway. The sooty smoke from her funnel trailed across the water to his nose; and the smell of kippers frying from the little crooked galley chimney.

Then the first merchant-ships were sweeping round

the river-bend from Jarrow. A little collier first, with a blue funnel and her sides streaked with rust. Coal for Battersea Power Station. No guns, not even a Lewis gun. The *Emma B* of London.

The next one was better. A ten-thousand-tonne tanker, painted nearly all grey, except for one big patch of red lead where the shipyard painters hadn't had time to finish her. Big six-inch gun on her stern, with a smaller gun above and behind it on a high round platform, still only painted with red lead. Anti-aircraft gun . . . the *Esso Venturer* of Milford Haven.

Then a Norwegian, with huge letters twenty feet high painted along her hull: NORGE. In the hopes that the U-boat captain would see it through his periscope and not torpedo her. Some fat chance. The stinking cowardly U-boats would torpedo anything, especially if it was full of women and children, like the *Arandora Star*.

Granda appeared at his elbow, puffing on his pipe, not saying anything. Together they waved to every passing ship, and always somebody waved back, even if it was just the cook in his white hat, tossing a bucket of potato peelings over the side. Some ships sounded their sirens in greeting, making Sonny tingle from head to foot with pride. Battle-wagons, he thought, battle-wagons going to the War. And he was part of it.

Finally, a smart sloop, the *Black Swan*, a real warship with three 4.7-inch guns in turrets. An Aldis lamp blinked from her bridge.

'Goodbye and good luck.' Granda spelt out the flashing light.

'Is that for us?' asked Sonny, awed.

'Aah doubt it,' said Granda. 'More like C-in-C Tynemouth.'

They watched the last ship, till she turned outside the piers, heading south.

'You're just like your mam was,' said Granda. 'Every time yer dad brought her here, when they were courting, she'd be up here like a flash, borrowing my old binoculars. Wantin' to knaa everything about the ships. What sort they were, where they were goin'. She often said Aah could leave her up here all day wi' binoculars and a packet o' sandwiches, an' she'd die happy. Aye, she was always happy when she came here . . .'

It should have hurt, horribly. But somehow it didn't. Maybe it was just the lovely evening, the soft golden light, lying over everything. Or maybe it was finding a place where Mam had always been happy. Or discovering he was just like she'd been . . . Suddenly he felt that Mam was somewhere not too far away, perhaps even listening now to him and Granda talking.

He fell into a daydream. This harbour, with things happening all the time, things coming and going, was like a huge theatre. And all things, from the warships to the gulls fighting and squawking round the distant sewer-outlet, were actors. The newspapers were beginning to talk about 'the European theatre of war'. He'd never known what they meant, till now. Now he had his own theatre of war, and the best seat in the world . . . He explained this to Granda. Granda puffed on his pipe thoughtfully. He said at last, 'Mebbe we've got the best seat in the stalls, Sonny,

38

or mebbe we're on stage, really. Aah only hope the audience don't start throwing things . . .'

He dreamt that night he was back in the kitchen at Newcastle, and his mam walked in the door, smiling, with a shopping bag in each hand. He was so glad to see her, so glad it had all been a stupid mistake. But it threw him in a happy panic.

'Mam, where've you been? Everyone thinks you're dead. We had a funeral for you. Me dad's gone off to join the RAF. We'll have to tell him—'

But Mam smiled again, and raised a finger to her lips.

'Not yet, Sonny. It's a secret. Between you and me.'

'But *why*?'

'I've got to go on hiding from everybody for a bit. You mustn't tell anybody.'

Then she bent forward and kissed him, smiled a third time and went out the door, saying, 'I won't be long.'

'Mam, where you *going*?'

But she was gone, and he was awake, in the dark, in his room in the lookout tower, in the bunks the off-duty coastguards had used so long ago. He lay in the dark, hugging the memory of the dream to himself, warming himself with it, while it slowly faded. He felt desolate, that it was only a dream. And yet, even when it had dwindled to almost nothing, it was not quite nothing. Nothing could ever be quite so dark again.

Dad came home on leave. He arrived without warning one Saturday morning, looking like a military Christmas tree, hung with blue ammunition pouches and small-pack and big-pack, and a huge drooping kitbag on each shoulder.

'By Gum,' said Granda, 'ye've got more to carry than we had in 1914. Even an eagle couldn't fly wi' all that stuff hung round him!'

'Fly?' said Dad. 'Don't talk to me about *flying*. Aa've got as much chance of flying as a rubber duck.' His face was livid. 'I've been *posted*. Aero-engine conversion course. For qualified engine-fitters. They're trying to make me into a bloody mechanic. Aah knew Aah shouldn't ha' trusted that CO, smarmy swine. And Aah told him so, to his face.'

'Eeh, lad,' said Nana, getting up to hug him. 'Have you got yourself in trouble?'

'No,' said Dad. 'Aah've got meself these again.' He tapped the two stripes on his shoulder. 'Aah had to cut them off when Aah left Blackpool, and then when I got to me new unit, Aah had to sew them back on in a couple o' weeks. But they're still not paying me for them. You don't get paid for being a nanny an' a nursemaid.'

'Sit ye down an' I'll cook ye some breakfast,' said Nana.

'No chance o' air gunner then?' asked Granda, warily.

'Oh, promises, promises! Qualify at yer trade, and then you can apply to be an air gunner. Har, har, har. Aah knaa what's on their little minds. In charge of ground crew. Same job I was doing at Armstrong Siddeley's, only on a quarter of the pay. Aah might as well have stayed at home. Then Aah wouldn't have to salute young pups who don't know their arse from their elbow.'

'Aye, well,' said Granda. 'It'll be a long war, the way things are going at the moment. Mebbe you'll still get your chance. Meanwhile, at least your mother can sleep sound in her bed at nights, wi'out worrying about you all the time.'

After breakfast, Dad said, 'Coming for a walk along the cliffs, Sonny?' He went to the corner, where he had left his old air rifle, when he had gone into the RAF. It wasn't a kid's air rifle, a piffling little Diana. It was a huge black oily thing, foreign, too big for Sonny to use. Dad shoved an old, creased, oily box of slugs into his uniform pocket and they set off.

'There's no rats round here, Dad.' They used, in the old days, to go shooting rats in the abandoned shipyards down by the river.

'Aah'm not after rats this morning.' Dad was eyeing the sea-birds circling off the cliffs. Suddenly, he stopped, broke open the air-gun, and put a slug in it. Then he clicked it shut and raised it. Sonny watched the distant circling birds with horror. They were so beautiful, so free . . . which one of the seven . . . ?

The air-gun spat. The top gull seemed to leap two feet higher, in an explosion of white feathers, then it was falling like something you'd tossed off the cliff. It hit the muddy brown flat rocks with a thump, and bounced twice, and then was still. Loose feathers blew away across the rocks into the Tyne.

Dad broke and clicked the gun again. Another gull, further away, fell in crying ruin. Far out on the rocks, it moved feebly; it was still alive.

Dad loaded the gun a third time. He was a terrifying shot; he always had been. He never missed.

A third graceful bird died on the wing. And a fourth. And a fifth. Sonny could not bear it; he closed his eyes. And then a rage leapt inside him. He opened his eyes, and saw the gun raised again, and reached up and pulled the barrel down.

'Dad! They're *British* seagulls!'

He could hardly recognize Dad's face, it was so twisted. He braced himself for the blow that he knew was coming. For once he didn't care.

But Dad only swung round. They were right underneath the huge monument that had been raised to Admiral Collingwood, the great Geordie admiral who had fought alongside Nelson at the Battle of Trafalgar. It was forty feet up to the Admiral's white legs, maybe eighty feet up to his great white face . . .

The air-gun spat. Tiny white fragments of stone flew off from the Admiral's nose. And Sonny knew that Dad had been aiming for the nose.

'And that's what Aah think o' perishin' officers,' said Dad. 'They're aall the flippin' same. Featherin' their own nests.'

Sonny was utterly appalled; it was worse even than the seagulls. Admiral Collingwood was a hero, almost a God to Geordies.

But it seemed to have satisfied something in Dad. He did not load the gun again. Instead, he said, 'That murderin' Dornier been back?'

'No, Dad, no. There's been nothing. Not even any air-raids. Ask Granda . . .'

'Well, keep your eyes skinned.' Dad looked at his

42

watch on his lean, black-haired wrist. 'Nigh eleven. Time for a drink.'

It was not a happy weekend. Sonny spent it desperately trying to remember Dad as he had been before the War, before Mam died. Always making things he'd been, wonderful things, galleons with all sails set, wireless cabinets, even a whole greenhouse. He'd always whistled happily as he worked; always let Sonny help. They'd been mates. Playing football on the beach in the holidays. Dad had been a really great player, slim and fast, not fat and clumsy like some lads' dads, who made themselves laughing-stocks.

And, much earlier, Dad picking Sonny up and throwing him to the ceiling, and catching him at the last moment, as he came down again. And laughing, always laughing.

Dad had been so much fun.

But somehow Sonny knew now that Dad's darkness had always been there; just hidden away underneath Mam's light.

5

The moment he got to school, he knew something was up. The boys in the playground watched him come, and muttered in little huddles. The pushier girls demanded to know what was going on, but the boys only shook their heads, and smiled rather nasty smiles. All during the first lesson there were glances and mutterings, and the girls getting cross because no one would tell them. Miss Black, the teacher, noticed, complained in a querulous Monday-morning sort of way.

'I don't know what's got into you this morning.'

But Sonny knew he was the target. Every eye was on him; faces looked curious, appalled, and some downright vicious. And when the bell went, for break, Jackie Robinson vanished without a word. Sonny drifted out to look for him, but stayed clear of hidden corners, in the middle of the yard, where the teacher on duty could see him. Podger Armstrong's gang were gathering round him in force.

Finally, they all came across. Sonny eyed Podger's heavy leg muscles under his shorts, his big, beefy hands, his bulging, muscly face, his thick lips, open mouth that never had any expression, his little eyes like blue marbles.

'Hey, Prudhoe?'

'What yer want?' Sonny tried to keep his voice calm, neither cringing nor hostile.

'Is yer dad an air gunner yet? What about that machine gun bullet?'

'Haven't got any. He has to train to be a mechanic, before he can apply to be an air gunner . . .'

'War'll be over afore then!' That got a hostile laugh from the crowd. But not much of one. There had to be more to it than this. But the blow, when it came, took his breath away.

'Where's yer mam, then?'

He pulled himself together and just said,

'She's dead,' in a flat voice.

'When did she die?'

'Last December.' Podger was grinning slyly, drawing it out.

'I heard she was a bit more than dead. How did she die?'

'She was killed by a bomb.' A terrifying tear tickled the corner of one eye, and he blinked rapidly, to absorb it down his nose. If he cried . . .

'I heard she was blown to bits. I heard they never found nothing of her.'

'That's a lie.' Anger was coming to his help now. 'That's a lie. She was buried like anybody else. I saw her coffin.'

Podger laughed, delighted. 'You don't want to let that fool you. They have a coffin even if there's nothing left. They put sandbags in it, to comfort the bereaved. My father said so, and he's in the ARP.'

'That's a lie! How would *he* know?'

'It's the talk of the ARP. It's all over Newcastle. She was blown into little, tiny bits. The birds pick the bits off the rooftops an' eat them. Your mum's a dicky-bird's breakfast!'

He had thrust his grinning face to within inches of Sonny's.

He had no sense of his own danger.

Sonny didn't do anything. His mind didn't tell him to do anything. His body simply exploded. He had a vague memory of his hand clawing out for Podger's nose and eyes, and then the world was just full of whirling limbs and a red mist. It went on and on. He felt pains, far off, in his hands, in his knees on the hard ground. But they were nothing as the terrible forces flowed through him.

And then there were hands holding his wrists, very strong hands that he couldn't shake off. He made an attempt to bite the wrist of the hand that held his right fist, his punching fist, imprisoned.

'Prudhoe!' yelled a man's voice, a voice of dire authority. He opened his eyes from near-blind slits, and saw his headmaster's face. How had Podger Armstrong turned into the headmaster? Where *was* Podger Armstrong?

There were three other teachers, bending over someone on the ground. A heavily muscled boy's leg stuck out absurdly between Miss Beaver's shiny black shoes. Podger's leg. He'd know it anywhere. But the noise that rose above the teachers' worried mutters wasn't Podger's voice. It was like a pig's squeal, only the pig was saying words that Sonny couldn't make out. Saying them over and over.

The headmaster, still holding his wrists, shook Sonny. As one might shake a puppy that had done something wrong on the carpet. Then he said, 'Come with me, Prudhoe,' in a dire voice, and, still holding one wrist, began to drag Sonny into school. As he went, he heard the kids muttering.

'He *bit* Podger Armstrong.'

'He tried to bite the Head.'

'He *hit* Miss Beaver. Did you hear her yell?' That was the girls, high and shrill and outraged. And yet a gloating in their voices, telling how much they'd loved the drama. Oh, their little tongues wouldn't stop for a week, now. It'd be all round the town . . .

The only comfort was one boy's voice, muttering,

'Old Podger had it coming . . .' But another boy's voice said,

'Hell, I know. But that Prudhoe's a loony. He was foaming at the mouth, like a loony out of Morpeth. He's not *human*.' Again, that gloating awful excitement.

The Head took Sonny into the cloakroom. For some reason he ran the cold tap into a sink, then plunged Sonny's hands into the water and held them there. He said, in a voice that almost cracked, 'You've got to cool down, Prudhoe. You've got to cool *down*!'

Sonny looked at his hands under water, the way they darkened and seemed to bend at the wrists, in a totally unnatural way. He saw, without much surprise, that they were bleeding from the knuckles; twists of pink coming up at him through the clear clean water.

'Whatever got into you?' asked the Head in a shocked condemning voice, from over Sonny's head.

'Please, sir.' Sonny's voice was developing a crazy quaver now, so he could hardly get the words out. 'Please, sir, he said my mother was blown to bits.

That little birds ate her on the roofs. That there was just sandbags in her coffin.'

'Dear God in Heaven,' said the Head, and his voice was quite changed. He let go of Sonny's wrists; and Sonny straightened up to see the Head standing with his eyes screwed up tight shut. Then the Head opened them again. But his face stayed very pale.

'You'd better come to my room. I'll get out the first aid kit.'

The Head's hands were surprisingly deft and gentle with the Elastoplast. Then he felt Sonny's head, under his hair.

'You've got a bump the size of an egg, there. Do you hurt anywhere else?'

'All over, sir.' Different parts of his body were coming back to life and hurting; like the different parts of a battleship reporting in to damage-control, after it had been in action.

'Elastoplast on both knees, I think.' The Head knelt on the floor, at Sonny's feet. 'Sit down in that chair, so I can see better.'

'Sir, it's not true, is it? About my mam?' Sonny heard his treacherous voice wandering all over the place. If only the Head could make it all right again . . .

The Head squatted back on his haunches, thought long. Then he said sadly, 'I don't know, Sonny. It could be true. I've heard stories . . . Sonny, she wouldn't have felt a thing. It must have happened in . . . the twinkling of an eye.'

'I know. But where *is* she? I want to know where she *is*. Is she in Newcastle Cemetery or . . . ?' He heard himself screeching.

'Do you believe in God, Sonny?'

'I don't know . . . I'm not sure. I *think* so.'

'Well, all I can say is that I'm sure she isn't in Newcastle Cemetery, Sonny. *Nobody's* in Newcastle Cemetery. You have a choice, Sonny. She's either in Heaven, or nowhere at all.'

It was a cold, hard comfort. But it worked. He could bear to think of Mam in Heaven; he could bear to think of her nowhere at all, though it was very hard. As long as she wasn't in the bellies of little birds, or bird-mess on some roof.

He looked at the Head's concerned face. He was a nice man; though he did cane people, he was fair. And now the Head was treating him like a man. He tried his stiff face in a ghost of a smile.

'Thanks, sir.'

'That's all right, Sonny. Now, Sonny, you're never going to do this kind of thing again, are you? I mean, Armstrong in the yard . . .'

'Is he hurt bad, sir?'

'Nothing he won't get over, given time. I doubt he'll be in school tomorrow . . . Now will you promise me, never again?'

Sonny thought hard. Until today, he could have made that promise, with an open heart. But now, he hardly knew himself. Suppose this strange, wild beast in him jumped out again?

'If they'll leave me alone, sir . . .'

'I'm quite sure, after this, they'll leave you alone.' The Head allowed himself the tiniest hint of a smile.

'Are you going to cane me, sir?'

'A boy in your state is in no condition to be caned. I shan't cane you, and I shan't cane Armstrong. I'm

49

sure you've both learnt a great deal . . . I rather feel like caning Armstrong's parents . . . no doubt I shall be seeing them, but I shall restrain myself.'

The handbell sounded for the end of break. Very late. The hubbub of voices, thronging back into school. High with excitement, all talking about Sonny, interrupting each other with squeaks and yells.

'One part of me wants to run you home,' said the Head. 'But we've only got my car, and I think I ought to run Armstrong to the hospital for some attention . . . I don't like to think of you walking home . . . it will be painful. Suppose you go back to your class and I'll run you home at the end of school.'

Sonny hesitated. All those eyes on him, all that muttering . . .

'Best to face them now,' said the Head. 'It will only get harder if you put if off. By tomorrow morning, otherwise, they'll have turned you into Count Dracula. Go on, there's a good lad, Sonny! Show them you're still *human*. You might even turn into a hero. Only, when you're a hero, Sonny, be *careful*.'

'OK, sir.' Sonny went.

When he opened the door, the whole class turned and stared. There was an awful hush. Sonny did feel like Count Dracula.

Then Miss Black said, 'Sit down, Sonny. We haven't got all day. It's maths. We're doing long division . . .'

And Jackie Robinson moved up the double desk to let him in, and smiled, and it seemed to be all right.

That night, Mam came to him in a dream. She looked just like she always had, smiling, in her headscarf.

'They said you were blown to bits!'

She smiled harder, spun round like she used to when she was showing off a new dress, to show him she was all of one piece. It comforted him.

'Where . . . where do you *live*?'

'Nowhere and everywhere, Sonny. But I hear what you say. I see what you do. I know what you think . . .'

'Podger Armstrong . . .'

'You don't want to worry your head about Podger Armstrong. He's a fool.'

'You'll go off again, in a minute.'

'Yes.'

'Why do you always go off?'

'I have things to do. But I'll come back and see you again. You know that.'

'Yes.'

And then she was gone, and he was awake, listening in the dark for the comforting sound of Granda's snores next door.

But afterwards, listening to the sound of the waves on the rocks, it was all right.

At school, nobody spoke to him except Jackie Robinson. And even Jackie Robinson was full of sly painful questions. Had he ever gone mad before like that? Had any of his family ever been put in Morpeth? Sonny gave him savage, abrupt denials, that made him back away and go pale.

And then came the morning when Podger Armstrong returned, brought by his mother. He was still wearing various bits of sticking plaster, and Mrs Armstrong came right into the classroom and talked to Miss Black, and went on and on about bullying, and kept looking round the room trying to spot which one Sonny was. But Sonny put his desk lid up, and was very busy tidying out his books. Mrs Armstrong went on and on, and called Podger by his real name, Cuthbert, which didn't do him any good, because titters began to simmer behind desk lids.

Finally, Miss Black began to walk to the door, drawing Mrs Armstrong away with her, out towards the school entrance.

That was when Podger made his bid to get back power; which was his big mistake. He shouted across the room to Sonny,

'I'll get you for that, Prudhoe! Just you wait!'

But somehow it lacked all conviction. Something made Sonny take two quick steps towards him . . . Next second, Podger was in full flight for the door, shouting,

'Mam, Mam!'

The whole classroom rocked with laughter. Kids banged their desk lids up and down with sheer glee. The idol had feet of clay, and had fallen for ever.

Sonny was very tempted to go after him, and give him another good bashing. Then he remembered the Head's warning, about being careful when he was a hero. And sat down demurely and began to tidy his books again. So that when Miss Black reappeared, dragging Podger by the shoulder, he could give her an innocent, enquiring look.

'Hallo, *Cuthbert*,' chorused the class.

'Have yer lost yer Mam, *Cuthbert*?'

It was a long time before poor Miss Black could restore order.

At break, the boy who'd been Podger's lieutenant drifted across to Sonny.

'Hey, Prudhoe, when you get those bullets off your dad, can I swop you one?'

'We'll see,' said Sonny coolly. 'We'll see.'

But he still worried whether he might be going mad. Or was he just a chip off the old block, like Granda said?

6

They were planting early potatoes. Granda dug a long trench, and then filled it with horse manure he'd scrounged from the Co-op Dairy stables, where he had an old mate. Then Sonny went along the row, planting the seed potatoes a foot apart, careful to set them the right way up. They were sprouting already, so he had also to be careful not to break off the delicate, new, white shoots. He liked the crinkly wrinkly feel of the potatoes, and he liked the smell of the crumbling horse manure. It was a friendly smell, not like what cows and pigs did.

It was a silent evening, cool and grey. Even the riveters upriver seemed to be taking a rest; except one working late in Jarrow, far off as a summer insect. So when Sonny accidentally knelt too hard on one Elastoplasted knee, and said 'ouch', it seemed to echo round the garden. He looked up quickly to see if Granda had noticed. Granda was busy lighting his pipe; it was just dusk enough for the match to illuminate in yellow the wrinkles in his cheeks.

'Bin in the wars, then?' asked Granda, shaking out the match till it gave off a little column of smoke.

'Yeah.'

'Yer nana noticed. She was aall for makin' a fuss, in case you'd been bullied. But Aah could tell from the look on yer face you hadn't been bullied. So Aah

54

reckoned you'd tell us in yer own good time, if you wanted to.'

'You oughta seen the other lad. He had to go to hospital.'

Granda cackled evilly, then broke off into a fit of coughing, as the smoke from his pipe went the wrong way.

'Aah told you – chip off the old block! What had he done – pinched yer best glass-alley?'

'Said things about Mam.'

'Aye,' said Granda, heavily. 'It's amazing how bad news travels. You'd think folks'd have more to do, worrying about the War.'

'Granda?'

'Aye?'

'Was it wrong? I *bit* him.'

Granda puffed on. Then took out his pipe and said, 'Aah once knew a Swedish feller had a piece of his ear bitten off, in a brawl down the Bullring.'

'What happened to the man that bit him?'

'The magistrate bound him over to keep the peace – the piece of the ear he'd bitten off, Aah suppose!'

They both laughed; the tension went. Then Granda said, 'Aah don't hold wi' bitin' meself. But Aah expect the lad was bigger than you?'

'Yeah, a lot. The form bully.'

'Well, you got to stand up for your womenfolk, Sonny. Man who can't do that, he's not worth calling a man. That's why yer dad's off into the RAF. Not that he's got a hope in hell of finding that Jerry. But he couldn't live wi' himself if he didn't *try*. Now, we've got three more rows to do, afore it's dark . . .'

They were just finishing when Nana came home all

in a fluster, saying that Mrs Jobling had said that her husband had heard that Hitler had invaded Norway and Denmark.

They hurried inside, and turned on the radio to see if there was any news. But the dance-bands that played, and the comedians who cracked jokes seemed never to have heard a word about Norway, which was very irritating. Granda got down his old atlas.

'Aah always thought that Hitler was a fool, and now Aah knaa he is. Look at Norway, Sonny. The coast's two thousand miles long, and the country's hardly five miles across, most of it. Even if Hitler wins – and them Norwegians is hard beggars – they used to be the Vikings – how can he hold on to a country that shape? He puts a handful of men every mile – that's ten thousand men. And no man can watch twenty-four hours a day – they'll have to work shifts like yer dad – that's thirty thousand men, just to stand sentry. We could land on that coast *anywhere*, at the cost of doin' in a few Jerries. The beggar's mad, Aah tell yer.'

Anxiously, in spite of Granda's words, they settled down to wait for the nine o'clock news.

Sonny leaned on the rail of the watchtower, a few weeks later, and thought how right Granda had been. Jerry had paid for Norway. Half his fleet gone to the bottom of the sea. Heavy cruiser, two light cruisers, twelve destroyers. And little HMS *Glow-worm*, British First World War destroyer, had taken on two German destroyers and a pocket-battleship single-handed, and sunk one destroyer and damaged the other, and then, to crown it all, had *rammed* the pocket-battleship, putting it in dry-dock till the end of the War. Granda said the Jerries were good seamen, but no match for the Royal Navy. Same in the Last Lot. They'd claimed they'd won the Battle of Jutland, but they never showed their noses again, till they sailed to scuttle themselves in Scapa Flow, for very shame.

As he waved the convoy out that night, Sonny felt great. Britannia rules the waves, he sang to himself. Then got Dad's letter out of his pocket. An oddly subdued letter.

'*Saw the CO again. No luck. No vacancies in the air gunnery school. So he says, and I can't argue. One bit of good news – he says I might soon get paid for my stripes. That'll be another half-crown on Nana's allowance, anyway, which I'm sure she can do with, trying to raise a growing lad. We're working on Merlin engines now. Rolls-Royce, the best. Big as an Austin-Seven car. Lovely workmanship – a thousand horsepower. They go in Spitfires and Hurricanes. As powerful as fifty old Armstrong-Siddeley cars! I'll bet those old Spitfires can shift! Be a good lad . . .*'

He heard Nana calling him for supper. He thought her voice sounded a bit funny. He folded up the letter and ran downstairs, and found Nana and Granda sitting each side of the table staring at each other in silence.

'What's up?'

Granda looked up, and for once he looked pale and lost.

'That beggar's invaded Holland and Belgium,' he said. Sonny had no need to ask who that beggar was. 'The Dutch'll flood their canals, and that might hold him up a bit . . . but . . .'

'There's the British Expeditionary Force,' said Sonny stoutly. 'They'll stop him . . . and there's the French!'

'Aah hope so,' said Granda. 'But Jerry on land's a lot different from Jerry at sea. Royal Navy's not goin' to be much help this time.'

He was helping Granda hoe up the potatoes they had planted so long ago. They were huge plants now, with thick curling luscious leaves.

'Why we burying them, Granda?'

'It's the bit underground that makes the little new potatoes. The more underground, the more potatoes.'

'Oh.' Sonny stared at them hopelessly. There was no help in potatoes, however many, when all the world was going wrong. The news was terrible. It had been terrible for weeks. Strategic withdrawals, shortening the defence line. The French 75s knocking out hundreds of German Panzers. Our lads are in good spirits, high morale . . . But there were always more Panzers. There was the word '*Blitzkrieg*' – the lightning-war. Holland had surrendered, after Rotterdam was bombed flat. Now the Belgians had surrendered. Hitler was unstoppable. Those Stuka dive-bombers screaming down from the sky, bombing everything to bits. French roads blocked with refugees. The little British Expeditionary Force, retreating, retreating, lost with Lord Gort somewhere near Dunkirk. Funny name for a French town, Dunkirk... sounded more Scottish, the brown church.

Granda finished hoeing; surveyed the finished furrows, with the tips of the plants sticking out of the top, looking lost and helpless and buried. 'Aye, they'll have to take their chance...'

But suppose Hitler won? What chance would the potatoes have then? Probably some man in jack-boots with a swastika on his arm would come goose-stepping up to just take them away. To feed the Herrenvolk...

It was then he thought he heard a plane. Out to sea. He looked up at the fat, uncaring, sunlit clouds and saw nothing. The sound seemed to have gone, and then it came again, the maddening way it does. It wasn't the steady drone of a British plane; he heard plenty of those, these days. No, it chugged, changed. Again, he seemed to lose it, as the wind dropped. Then it came a third time, making the pit of his stomach sink. It was a sound he remembered.

The sound that had killed Mam.

He scanned everywhere, wildly. Everywhere a plane might be, could be. Nothing. Yet the sound was quite loud now; though Granda hadn't noticed it yet. Maybe he was getting deaf, like Nana said. He was just standing there lighting his pipe.

Was the plane *behind* the clouds? No, it was lower, the sound; beneath the clouds. A secret weapon? An invisible plane?

He despaired and dropped his eyes to the sea instead. And then he saw it. A tiny dot, just above the sea, coming in between the piers. Coming in so low it seemed below the tops of the lighthouses. The setting sun winked on its front canopy.

'*Granda!*' He pointed.

Granda took the pipe out of his mouth and said, 'The cheeky so-and-so!'

'Granda, it's *German*.'

'How can you tell?'

'The engines.'

But Granda just went on staring at it. He just couldn't believe a Jerry could be there, where the gulls flew every day, and the fishing boats went out of harbour.

The plane changed course, slightly, to follow the bend of the river. It was hardly its own length above the water. Now Sonny could see the ripples it was making, on the smooth surface of the harbour, almost like a boat. As it grew nearer, he was getting more and more of a side view.

'Twin tails,' he whispered, 'twin engines. Separate bomb-aimer's window. Flying Pencil. Granda, it's him, it's *HIM*!'

It laid itself out before his eyes, as if proud of its monstrous devil-shape. The long thin body, mottled green on top, pale blue beneath, like a hideous insect. The spinning shining discs of the propellers. The very heads of the pilot and gunners, black dots. And as he watched, it dipped suddenly towards the water.

'Crash, bastard, *crash*!' he screamed. 'Bastard, bastard, *bastard*!'

But flaps moved delicately on the back edge of its wings, and tail, and it rose again to its original height.

The black crosses, edged with white; the swastika on the tails . . .

'Why don't they fire at it?' he screamed. 'Are they all *asleep*?' For the plane was passing now, invulnerable as a ghost. Over the little hut on the end of Lloyd's Hailing Station, past the Fish Quay where the armed trawlers lay . . . it was almost invisible now, against the blue haze upriver. As it turned, south towards the Jarrow bend, its wings winked once, and then it was gone, as if it had never been.

'He'll be photographing the ships in the river,' said Granda at last.

And then the siren went.

Nana came to the door, and shouted for them to come down the cellar.

'Haad yer whisht, woman,' said Granda. 'It's only one on his own, tekkin' photographs. He's gone up Newcastle by now.

'They'll get him!' shouted Sonny. 'They'll get him when he comes back.'

'Mebbe,' said Granda. 'At that height they can't shoot at him wi'out hitting the houses . . .'

'Is them machine guns?' said Nana, coming up to join them, wiping her hands on her pinny.

'No, woman, them's riveters. They're still working on the ships. They've not noticed. You've been hearing riveters aall yer life . . .'

But Sonny was not sure. One was too loud and slow for a riveter . . .

'Here's the beggar back,' said Granda, shading his eyes. 'Not taken him long to do his business.' Now there were more loud slow riveters . . .

The Jerry, if possible, was even lower. The ripples

61

followed beneath him as if they were the wake of some ghost-boat. Once, as he neared, it seemed to Sonny that one propeller touched the water, in a glint of white foam. Like when swallows skim low over water in the evening, taking a drink.

'Crash, bastard, crash!'

But again the little flaps moved on the tails, and the Jerry recovered. He was so close you could see the pilot's face, the goggles. His wing lifted, showing the blue underside, as he banked to miss their own cliff, the house. The sound of the engines was deafening.

There were three ear-splitting bangs. The cliff below their feet erupted mountains of soil and stones. Sonny's eyes were full of stuff, his nostrils full of a Guy Fawkes' smell.

'Geddown!' Granda's huge hand hit him in the shoulders, knocking him flat.

By the time he had rubbed the dust out of his eyes, Granda was peering over the garden wall, out between the piers.

'Gone,' he said. 'Got clean away.'

'He *bombed* us!' shouted Nana angrily. 'Why did he bomb *us*?'

'Them wasn't bombs,' said Granda in disgust. 'He was long past. Them was ours. Our side. Shells. Some beggar can't shoot straight. Come to that, none of them beggars can shoot straight.'

They got up, and dusted themselves off. Nana said, 'They coulda killed us.'

'Them gunners couldn't shoot straight in the Last Lot, either. Lot more dangerous than the Jerries.'

There were four more loud bangs, making them jump.

'The Castle,' said Granda in disgust. 'Who they trying to fool? He's out of range.' The German plane, the tiniest of dots, vanished as they looked at it. The shells from the Castle fell harmlessly into the sea, far out, puny. The bangs were a very long time rolling back over the gentle waves.

Then three planes roared overhead. Hurricanes, from Usworth.

'Too slow to catch cold!' shouted Granda after them. 'I hope they're a bit sharper over Dunkirk.'

A terrible fear was sweeping through Sonny. It paralysed him, standing there staring down at the newly buried potatoes. Mr Chamberlain, the Prime Minister, had been sacked, because he was a flop.

Suppose things didn't get better? Suppose Mr Churchill was a flop as well? Suppose all the British were flops. Like the Poles, the Dutch, the Belgians . . .

Just for a sneaking second he wondered, if you behaved yourself, would the Gestapo leave you alone? If you volunteered to join the Hitler Youth . . . ?

Then he heard Granda say, 'Aye well, we always lose every battle but the last one.'

He just hoped Granda was right.

Supper was a silent meal. They'd heard the nine o'clock news. The British Army were withdrawing to prepared positions round Dunkirk.

'A last stand, mebbe,' said Granda. 'Well, we held them at Mons. We shot so fast that day, Jerry thought we all had machine guns. But they didn't have no

Panzers in those days. Reckon a rifleman's not much cop against a Panzer . . .'

'Never mind aboot Dunkirk,' said Nana. 'I'm worried aboot here. If the so-an'-so's can fly in and out like that, whenever they feel like it, nobody can sleep safe in their beds.'

'Oh, Aah wouldn't worry aboot that, woman. They won't be all as smart as that feller tonight. He's an old hand, that one. Knew what he was doin'. An ace, mebbe, like von Richthofen, the Red Baron . . .'

'Did you ever see von Richthofen, Granda?'

'Aye, we saw him once or twice. Bright red Fokker Triplane, he flew. Him and his Flying Circus, they was painted all colours – real bonnie, blue and yellow stripes, some of them. But the bullet came, that had his number on it, just the same. Chased a young lad too close to the Aussie lines, south of us. But he died like an ace. Landed his plane perfect, even though he had a bullet right through him. They tore his plane to bits for souvenirs, then gave him a funeral with full military honours, firing squad an' all. Just like he was one of our own. Aah'm glad he went that way, and not as a flamer . . .'

'What's a flamer, Granda?'

'When they catch fire. Burn all the way to the ground. Some o' them used to bail out wi'out a parachute, to get away from the flames. Clean death.'

'Hadn't parachutes been invented?'

'Aye, but the Top Brass reckoned a parachute would make them into cowards. So they had none.'

Sonny renewed his attack on his fried sausage with fresh vigour. He had something new to hope for. That

64

the man who had killed his mother would end up a
flamer. A flamer straight down into Hell . . .

'Granda?'

'Aye?'

'Von Richthofen . . . he never killed a *woman*?'

'Not that Aah ever heard of.'

Granda watched him thoughtfully. You never knew
what was going on in the minds of the young . . .

'Dear Dad,
 We have seen him. He flew up the river and
out again, and nobody could hit him at all.
Granda says he is an old hand, an ace like von
Richthofen. I am sending you a drawing of
exactly what he looked like, so you will know.'

The drawing took him all day, between listening to
the news bulletins. The news was a bit better. The
men were coming home from Dunkirk. By the train-
load. Lots of little ships, trawlers, coasters, even
yachts, were going across to fetch them home. It was
going to be all right after all.

So he made the drawing his greatest masterpiece
yet. Copied out of the aircraft-recognition book, but
ten times the size. He inched his pencil across the
paper, tongue sticking out of the corner of his mouth
with the effort. Then he coloured it in, exactly. The
green leopard-mottle on the top, the pale blue
underneath . . . It must all be exactly right. It was a
pity the Jerries didn't have letters and numbers on
their planes, like the RAF had . . .

From outside the window, Granda watched him,
an unreadable expression on his face.

'*Dear Sonny,*

Well, here we are, somewhere else again. At least I've got my money for my stripes, and a little bit of paper saying I'm fit to be let near an aeroengine. They tried to post me to the north of Scotland, working on old Lysanders. I ask you, with all the trouble that's coming! I went and told him straight. I asked him where the hot spot was going to be and he gave a nasty laugh and said, "Still trying to get yourself killed, Prudhoe?" So I told him about your mam, and that wiped the smile off his face. He said I could swop with young Bert Finch, who's got a wife and four kids to worry about and wants a soft option. Can't say where I am now, but we're not short of a bit of white chalk round here, the cliffs are full of it.

I am in charge of a Hurricane, with a rigger to see to the rest of the plane and two armourers to load the guns. I don't think much of the pilot they've given me. He doesn't look much older than you, but talks like he's got a plum in his mouth. Rich daddy, little sports car, and never done a hand's turn in his life, I reckon. Thinks the War's a game. Can't see him lasting long, once the balloon goes up.

There's another pilot I've got my eye on. A Pole, though he speaks good English. They say he fought the Jerries over Warsaw, in an old PZL bi-plane, and knocked down two of them. And he got two more in France. He's the lad for me, though he never says anything.

They say the Jerries killed his wife and kid. So that's a bond between us.

Don't worry if you don't hear from me, the next few weeks. I reckon we're going to be a bit busy with old Adolf.

Thanks for the picture – very good. I showed it to our Intelligence Officer. He says it's the oldest kind of Flying Pencil, the one the Jerries used in Spain with the Condor Legion, that bombed all those little bits of bairns to pieces at Guernica. That gentleman seems to make a habit of it, doesn't he? Ah well, we'll see. God is not mocked.

Take care of Granda, and give Nana a kiss and a big hug for me.

Your loving Dad.'

Sonny felt very proud about his drawing. He really felt part of the War Effort.

7

Sonny slept late that morning, and awakened hot and sweating to the sound of a trumpet. Such a fierce, braying trumpet, nothing like the bugles that sounded reveille or lights-out at the Castle every day, faint and sweet. No, this was a trumpet that called you to be harsh, to be brave. And from the crackling that went with it, it was on the wireless downstairs. Which was odd, because Nana and Granda never had the wireless on in the morning, so as to save the batteries.

Instantly, he knew something awful had happened. He ran downstairs in his pyjamas, refastening the cord as he went.

Nana and Granda were sitting on each side of the big, old radio, still as stones.

'What's up?'

'The French have surrendered to Hitler.'

'Oh, they *haven't*!' It was impossible. Sonny was outraged. The French had millions of soldiers left. The biggest tank in the world. That submarine, the *Surcouf* with great, huge guns. Dewoitines were faster than Spitfires... well, than Hurricanes, anyway. They *couldn't* have surrendered. The goodies never gave in to the baddies, no matter how hard things got. He had a sudden brainwave. 'Maybe the French only *pretended* to surrender? Then, when the Jerries left their trenches, they mowed them down...'

68

'That's a canny little idea,' said Granda, 'but Aah'm afraid not. We've lost our only friends, Sonny.'

'Good riddance to bad rubbish, Aah say,' said Nana. 'Them French is soft. Aall they think about, when they get into port, is drink and women. Dirty lot – Mrs Lambert says they haven't got a flush toilet to bless themselves with. Just a little hole in the ground at the bottom of their gardens, and then they put it all on their growing vegetables. What can you expect from people like that?'

'No,' said Granda, shaking his head vigorously. 'Aah won't have that. The French were good fighting men, the ones Aah knew. They held Verdun to the bitter end. "*Ils ne passerent pas*" was their motto. "They shall not pass." And they didn't. Not in the Last Lot they didn't. I blame them Panzers, and them Stukas. They say they're more than flesh an' blood can stand.'

'But General Gamelin had a *plan*!' shouted Sonny.

'Aye, but it's one thing havin' a plan, when you're safe behind your typewriter in your big château. Something else to carry it out when you're crawling through barbed wire.'

'So what do we do now?' yelled Sonny.

'Mr Churchill's speakin' on the radio tonight. Mebbe he'll have a few ideas.' He surveyed his only grandson's face and seemed to decide that even Mr Churchill wasn't quite enough. 'Ye can come up to the Castle wi' me this afternoon if you like. Aah'm away down the Quay to scrounge a bit of lemon sole for the Major.'

'Can we see the *guns*?'

69

'Aah expect the Major'll let you, if you're good. He'll get no more lemon sole out of me, otherwise.'

They walked up the hill to the Castle together. Granda moved faster than usual. Even though he carried a heavy straw bag in each hand, that dripped the smell of fish, and was crudely stamped in black 'Geo Hastie and Sons, Fish Merchants'. Granda's head was up, and his shoulders were back, and it seemed to Sonny he was like an old warhorse, sniffing the smoke of battle. And far away in his mind. Once he grunted, to no one in particular,

'Old Jerry never did like cold steel.'

Funny, he never made out he hated the Jerries like some people tried to. He seemed quite fond of them; like a farmer is fond of his pigs before he sends them to slaughter.

The sentry on the Castle gatehouse was like something out of a movie. 'Halt, who goes there?' The sharp, fixed bayonet waving in their faces; the little black hole at the end of the rifle that might blossom yellow flame at any moment, and blow your head off. The sentry's finger on the trigger . . .

'Now, Alf,' said Granda gently, pushing the point of the bayonet to one side with the tip of one finger. 'Steady on. It's my turn to buy a round at the Rock of Gibraltar.'

The sentry grinned sheepishly from under his tin hat. 'Only following orders, Mr Prudhoe. What you got in them bags?'

'Lemon sole for the officers; cod for the sergeants.'

'Lucky so-and-sos. Tinned beef stew for us *again*.' The sentry had a good sniff at the bags, as if he could

70

feed on that, then he withdrew his head reluctantly, and Sonny and Granda walked across to a low brick building, from which a not-very-nice cooking smell was coming. Granda knocked, and the greasiest man Sonny had ever seen came to the open door. His long apron must once have been white, but now, across his flat belly, it was dark-brown and transparent, like a chip-paper when you've eaten the chips. Further up and down, and on his cook's hat, there was still some off-white between the brown splashes. His thin pale arms were covered with faint blue tattoos. The left arm had a woman in a hood, with 'Mother Mary' underneath. The right arm had a skull and crossbones and 'Death Before Dishonour'. On his feet were the least shiny boots Sonny had ever seen, sooty black.

'Now, Scouse,' said Granda, 'I got some nice cod and sole, and this is my grandson Sonny.'

Scouse transferred his fish-slice to his left hand and offered Sonny five fingers as shiny, hot and greasy as fresh-cooked sausages.

'He looks like a lad that could do wi' a fried egg sandwich!' He cocked a questioning black eyebrow at Sonny. Beneath his cook's hat his blue-black hair stuck out in spikes stiff with grease.

Silently, Sonny nodded. Eggs were like gold; he hadn't had one for a fortnight.

'Come in.' All around in the semi-dark, more tall greasy figures, one singing, 'There'll be bird-shit over, the white cliffs of Dover . . .'

Scouse picked up an egg, from a vast cardboard tray of them, and rubbed it along the side of a huge frying pan, on a long stove so hot it felt like the sun. The egg sprayed across the pan, and immediately

71

frizzled brown. Scouse broke the yoke with a poke, flipped the egg over, then flipped it between two slices of thick white bread that had appeared in his other hand out of nowhere. It was like a conjuring trick.

'I'll bet old Hitler wishes he could have a fried egg sandwich as quick as that,' said Scouse. 'Bet he has to wait hours, wi' them long corridors at Berchtesgarten, an' when he gets it, it'll be stone-cold.'

'Thanks.' It burnt his mouth, but it was smashing. Granda and Sonny walked round the grass slope inside the ramparts.

'If them gunners are as quick wi' their shells as Scouse is with a fried egg, Aah reckon old Hitler's in for a rough time,' said Granda. Sonny just nodded. His mouth was too full and his eyes were watering.

Until they came to a huge black cannon, pointing out to sea. Even to Sonny, it seemed *incredibly* old-fashioned.

'No,' said Granda. 'That's not waiting for Hitler. That's still waiting for Napoleon. He never turned up in these parts, he had more sense. Mind you, a few foreigners came looking for trouble. The Saxons burnt the Roman signal station across the river, on the Lawe at Sou' Shields. An' the Vikings came to mek trouble, but they ran aground on Jarrow Slake, not knowin' the river was shallow there. Aall their boats was wrecked, and they were hunted down to the last man, an' they skinned *him* alive an' nailed his skin to the church door. It's still there, as far as Aah know, but it doesn't do much to keep the draught out . . .

'And the Scots had a go at us, once or twice, but

we killed their king at Neville's Cross. The Bishop of Durham's men did that.'

'*Bishop?*' It was not at all Sonny's idea of what bishops were for.

'Oh, terrible men they were, the Bishops of Durham. Hang a man as soon as bless him.'

'Was there always fighting here?'

'Always a castle of sorts. Pen-bal-Crag, the old Celts called it – they've found their bronze axe-heads here. Dug 'em up. A strong place, Pen-bal-Crag. Never been taken by the enemy.'

Now they were passing the towering ruins of the Priory. Lots of old gravestones, incredibly worn away by the wind and rain, but still bearing inscriptions like 'Tyne Pilot' or 'Master Mariner'. Sonny thought how nice it must be to have a big tombstone like that. A bit like passing the eleven-plus.

'Penny for them?' asked Granda.

'I was thinking how nice it must be, to be dead with honour,' said Sonny tremulously.

'Hadaway wi' ye,' said Granda. 'Better to be alive wi' honour. Come an' meet a friend of mine.'

They came to a clear and newly cut tombstone. To a Corporal Alexander Rollo, died aged eighty-something.

'He fought against Napoleon, when things were at their blackest. In Spain, when the great British General Sir John Moore got killed. But he came home safe, and lived long enough to hold me in his arms, when Aah was a babby. Died safe in bed, wi' all his children an' grandchildren round him. The great Sir John Moore died, but little Alexander Rollo came home. So, you see, don't be over-quick to be a dead

73

hero . . . ye might live to have grandchildren who'll think Old Hitler nowt but a bogeyman in a story-book. If a shell or bomb's got your number on it, it'll get you. And if it hasn't, it won't. And there's nowt you can do about it, so why worry?

'See that spit o' land there, sticking out into the river? That's called the Spanish Battery. Been waitin' for the Spaniards since 1588 – I don't think *they're* going to make it, either. Aye well, come and see the guns.'

They were stopped before they got to the guns by a corporal, who sent for a sergeant, who sent for the officer. But the officer only said, 'Morning, Mr Prudhoe, fetched us some nice lemon sole?'

'Aye. Aah was wonderin' if you'd show the laddo here your guns. Cheer him up, like! He's a bit down in the mouth about the French . . .'

The officer pulled an awful face. 'I think we're better off without them. One less thing to worry about. We know where we are now.'

'Aye,' said Granda. 'Aah know what ye mean.'

The officer showed Sonny everything. The ammu-nition-hoists that brought the shells up, from the magazines that were safely buried deep in the cliff. The huge brass breeches of the guns, that unscrewed and swung open like round doors, revealing a shiny dark round twisting tunnel you could look along and see blue sky at the far end. The telescopic sight, with its cracked rubber eyepiece, which showed a trawler plunging across it, sending out a huge plume of smoke that followed along behind it on the wind.

'You see the cross-shape inside the sight?' asked the officer. 'When that rests right across the middle of that trawler, you pull the lanyard, and the trawler gets blown to smithereens. You know how they get the lines of that cross so thin? They make them out of spider's webs . . .'

But to Sonny, the trawler wasn't a trawler, it was a Flying Pencil. He let the cross-hairs settle plumb on target, and vigorously pulled the lanyard.

'Warlike little devil, isn't he,' said the officer admiringly.

'Jerry bomber killed his mam,' mouthed Granda softly.

The officer shook hands with Sonny, and looked at him with solemn respect, as if he was suddenly a very important person indeed.

Then they set off back home for tea.

'Granda?'

'Aye?'

'Them guns – they had VR cut into them. Like they have on pillar-boxes. That's Queen Victoria, isn't it? Made in Queen Victoria's reign. They're *old*, aren't they?'

'Well, they were certainly here in 1915, when the German cruisers shelled Scarborough. But the Germans never dared come here, so them guns haven't been used very much. Just for practice. It's not age that wears guns out, but being used too often.'

But Sonny could hear the doubt in Granda's voice.

8

Mr Churchill's words still rang in Sonny's head. He mouthed them under his breath, as he carried the full watering can to Granda with both hands, his shoulders so pulled down with the weight he could hardly breathe. He never wanted to forget Mr Churchill's words.

'What General Weygand has called the Battle of France is over. It may be that the Battle of Britain is about to begin . . .' And even better, 'We shall fight them on the beaches and in the cities. We shall never surrender.' There were lots of other places Mr Churchill had said we would fight them, but he couldn't remember them all, which was *maddening*.

'Don't be all day wi' that waterin' can,' called Granda.

Just then, the gate clicked. He and Granda looked up. There was an Army officer walking up the path, followed by a weedy-looking civilian in a long grey mackintosh and trilby hat, carrying a briefcase. Somehow, it looked like trouble . . .

'Mr Prudhoe!' said the officer in a too-friendly tone. 'I think I've seen you at the Castle. I've certainly enjoyed your fish!'

'Aye,' said Granda, suspiciously. 'Well, get on wi' it!'

'We're setting up coastal defences. Roadblocks, barbed wire, anti-personnel mines, tank-traps . . .'

'Aye, well?'

'Well, I'm afraid your house is going to be outside the defences, Mr Prudhoe. We're taking the barbed wire straight across the castle cliff to the bottom of Prior's Park. Tank-traps on the pier-approach road, and a sentry-box. Even if we had the barbed wire to spare, your little headland is indefensible . . . We have to do the best with what we've got.'

'Aah see,' said Granda, a bit taken aback. 'Well, I expect we'll manage, like we've always done.'

'Well, it's not quite as simple as that. We'd like to move you. Evacuate you inland, where you'd be safe in the case of invasion. This gentleman can luckily allocate you an empty council house, which just happens to have fallen vacant . . .'

Granda's hands clenched into fists behind his back. 'Council house – *where*?'

The officer turned to the other man. Who did not look at Granda, but opened his briefcase and fiddled with papers inside.

'Eleven, Walnut Crescent,' he stammered.

'That'll be the *Ridges*,' said Granda in an awful voice. Sonny thought he might be going to hit somebody soon.

'Eer . . . yes. But a nearly new house . . . not built two years ago. All mod cons . . . electricity, gas, indoors flush toilet, water-heating back-boiler, large garden . . .'

'Full of tin cans an' rusty bikes wi' dead grass a yard high an' the front door half kicked in by drunks no doubt.'

77

'You're exaggerating, Mr Prudhoe,' said the man huffily.

'Putting *us* in wi' the riff-raff!' said Granda, almost in a whisper.

'Come, Mr Prudhoe, be reasonable,' said the officer. 'Some folk bombed-out down south haven't even got a roof over their heads—'

'I'd rather have no roof than live on the *Ridges* . . .'

'But . . . see it as an old soldier, Mr Prudhoe. If we could evacuate you, we could demolish your house to improve our field of fire . . . As it stands, your house would give excellent cover to the enemy as they land.'

'Demolish?' yelled Granda. '*Demolish?* Aah own every stick and stone of that house. Bought it with me Compen Money in 1926, when no other beggar would look at it. House and half an acre o' garden. That house has stood for nigh on two hundred year, rain an' shine. An' you want to *demolish* it?'

'Only in the National Interest. For the sake of the War Effort. This is no time for pettiness! The future of Britain is at stake.'

'An' so's the future of your fish supply,' shouted Granda. 'If you shift me from this house, that's the last fish you get. *Ever*. Aah'll not fetch it for you, and when Aah tell the lads down the Quay what you've done, nobody else will, either. You'll not get as much as a smell of fish for the rest of the War. You'll be back to corned beef hash, with your poor Tommies.'

'There's no need to make a *personal* issue of it, Mr Prudhoe!' But the officer suddenly looked doubtful, even a little wild. He was obviously thinking of the Major and his lemon sole. Granda seized his chance.

'Aah can assure ye that, come the Invasion, no Jerry will tek cover in *my* house. By the time they brek in, it'll be up in flames. Aah guarantee it. Jerry will get in over my dead body.'

'Aye, an' me an' all.' Nana now stood in her kitchen doorway, drying her hands on her apron. 'Aah'll buy a bottle o' vitriol and *blind* the beggars.'

The two men began to back away towards the gate.

'I'll have to consult the CO,' called the officer.

'That house on the Ridges'll be gone by the end of the week,' said the man from the council, spitefully.

'Good riddance to bad rubbish!' said Nana.

All three of them stood and watched the men walk away up the pier-approach until their heads vanished from sight under the clock tower.

Then Nana and Granda looked at each other a very long time.

'Aye well,' said Granda, 'we're on our own now, hinny. Just like poor old England. Aah'll need a few pounds out of the household kitty, Sarah.'

'You're not going to start your drinkin' again?'

'No, but we'll need sandbags an' tape for the windows, an' barbed wire an' posts. An' petrol, lots and lots o' petrol.'

The things Granda could scrounge were amazing. He knew so many people, and they all seemed to owe him a favour. The fence posts were already hammered in, inside the garden wall, and the barbed wire strung across them with big fat staples. Three strands, up to five feet from the ground. It would certainly keep out a cow or a horse . . .

'Aah know,' said Granda. 'It won't keep out Jerry

for long – he'll have wire-cutters. But it'll hold him up a couple of minutes, which is better than nowt. And Aah'll hang tin cans on it, so when Jerry starts cutting or crossing it, they'll jangle together and make a noise. That's what we did in the trenches.'

Sonny looked at the Old Coastguard Station with new eyes. It was becoming a fortress.

'But,' he said, looking at Granda, 'if the Army throw us out . . .'

'Divven't fret. Aah've had a word wi' the Major. He said he'd keep an open mind. We're past the worst wi' the Army, Aah reckon. Every day that passes, they get more used to the idea of an invasion . . . and more used to eating ma fish. They were just actin' hasty, in a panic. People do daft things, in a panic; they're calmer now.'

Then he nodded wisely to himself and said, 'Them walls is nigh three feet thick. An' the windows is small, because of the weather. We'll be safer down them cellars than in any flippin' Anderson shelter.'

Sonny thought of the deep, endless cellars, with their vaulted whitewashed brick arches, and nodded. Nobody else would be as safe, even up at the Castle.

'Next, we sandbag the windows,' said Granda. 'Aah couldn't get many sandbags, with there bein' a war on. But Aah've got the coalman fetching me a load of old coalsacks. They'll have to do. Stronger, anyway. Thing is, where we goin' to get the soil to fill 'em?'

He looked round his garden. Between the narrow paths, dressed each morning by Nana with cinders from the kitchen range, every patch bloomed like the Garden of Eden. The tall runner beans flamed out their scarlet flowers among the green, like tiny glittering fires. Cabbages fattened by the day. The leaves of turnips crisscrossed each other, fit to trip up any Jerry when he came, more than the barbed wire. Radishes, lettuces, swedes, cauliflowers . . .

'We can't destroy *food*,' said Granda. 'Not in wartime. And Aah don't want to dig up yer nana's dahlias, she'd never forgive me . . . Aye, the early potatoes'll have to be a bit earlier, that's all. At least Jerry won't get them, if he comes.'

So they filled two sacks with potatoes, and then they began to dig deeper, fill the sandbags with soil. At least Sonny held the mouths of the bags open, while Granda shovelled the sweet, damp soil in. It gathered in little heaps on Sonny's wrists, then slid off with a tickling feeling, as it dried. By knocking-off time, the hole in the potato patch was two feet deep, and there were little walls of sandbags across the two kitchen windows, set a few feet forward so that light could still come in. From inside the house, Nana watched them, as she stuck the sticky-tape on the inside of the tower windows. She stuck it in star-shapes, so that the tower gained a rather festive, Christmassy air, which was funny in the heat of July. But otherwise, the house looked more like a fortress than ever.

'Ye can't have a fort wi'out a flag, though,' said Granda. And he went into the house and emerged with a small bundle of red cloth, tightly wrapped round with cord. He attached it by toggles to the rope that eternally tapped against the flagpost, in the wind that never stopped blowing on the little headland. Granda drew on the ropes, and the bundle

81

went to the top of the flagpole, till it looked no bigger than Sonny's fist.

'Stand to attention,' said Granda sternly. 'Heels together, toes four inches apart.' Then he tugged on the rope, and the flag, on the third tug, broke free and blew bravely in the wind. There was a Union Jack in one corner, but the rest of the flag was just red, red as blood.

'Salute,' ordered Granda. 'Hup, one, two, three, down, one, two, three.' Then he added fervently, 'God Bless the King.'

'What flag is that?'

'The Red Ensign. Or the Red Duster, as we called it. That's the flag off my trawler, the *Sarah P.* Named after yer nana. Aah used to say that Sarah P was my boss at home, and the *Sarah P* was my boss at sea.'

At that point, Sarah P herself emerged, and said, 'What you doin' that for, ye daft old beggar? That flag'll make us a target for every Jerry that flies up the river.'

'Aye, mebbe,' said Granda. 'But that shows we don't think nowt o' Hitler.'

'Ye haven't got the sense ye were born with . . .'

'Wartime's not a time for sense. S'a time for *pride*.'

'Eeh, ye're as daft as a brush.' They were staring into each other's faces again, and there were tears glinting in Nana's blue eyes.

'What's for supper?' asked Granda. 'Ye've got plenty of new potatoes. Aah'll fetch some. No need to scrape them, they're so fresh the skins rub off wi' yer fingers.'

'One of these days, I'll rub off your skin wi' me fingers. When yer get fresh.'

They spoke so fiercely to each other, yet as they walked indoors side by side, their hands touched.

9

'By heck,' said Granda. 'If this hole gets much deeper, Aah'll need a ladder to climb out.'

'We're halfway up the last window,' said Sonny encouragingly. 'Twelve more sandbags to fill.' He looked across and up at the Old Coastguard Station. It looked blind, now, with not a window showing except in the three-storey lookout tower. Even the front and back doors had their walls of sandbags. He tied up the neck of the latest sandbag, and with an enormous heave, put it in the wheelbarrow.

'How often do Aah have to tell you,' said Granda, 'bend your knees to lift things, not your back. Ye'll give yerself a rupture.'

'What's a rupture?'

'Something ye won't have to worry about for a few years yet,' said Granda illogically.

'But . . . ?'

At that moment, the siren went, echoing oddly under the high clouds of sunset.

'Aah'm not stoppin',' said Granda. 'Half them sirens is false alarms. It's not bomber's weather. An' look how low them barrage balloons are . . .' Everyone thought when the balloons were low it meant no raid.

Granda went on gasping and shovelling. He was stripped to the waist and sweating. He had a hairy chest, but the hair was all grey and white and straggly, not like Dad's. His arms had huge muscles, but the skin hung off them in loose folds, and there were the long, blue veins like little snakes that branched and went on for ever. Sonny wondered how it must feel to be old . . .

'Nowt changes really,' said Granda. 'They might have their Spitfires an' their death rays an' such, but war's still some poor beggar digging a hole, when it comes down to it. To hide in, or do your business in, or bury somebody in. Little Corporal Rollo dug a hole for Sir John Moore, and a hundred years later, we're still at it. Gettin' very damp down here, too. One good rainstorm, ye'll have a pond to keep goldfish in. Aah know a feller can get us some nice goldfish . . .'

The bangs were so deafening that Sonny saw Granda's mouth opening and shutting, and couldn't hear a word of what he said. He glanced round wildly. Smoke was drifting away from the tip of Pen-bal-Crag. Then he saw the flash from the Castle guns, and his ears vibrated again. He could actually feel the little flaps of skin moving inside his ears.

'Geddown!' Granda's shout came faintly. A huge hand grabbed Sonny by the belt and yanked him down the hole.

Four little white clouds appeared in the sky in a ragged row, far out to sea. Explosions came rolling faintly back across the blue water, flecked with tiny waves. Then four more little puffy clouds, nearer land.

'There he is,' said Granda. 'The greenhorn.' The shape of a twin-engined plane appeared through the shellbursts, which were breaking up rapidly, and drifting south on the wind. 'That last feller, the Flying Pencil, knew what he was doin', keepin' so low. This feller's an idiot. He's scared, so he's flying too high, where the guns can get to him. They've got his range. God help him.'

The Castle guns fired a third time. The shell-bursts were behind the plane this time, but very near, making its wings rock wildly. Sonny could see it was not a Flying Pencil; too fat, with a rounded body like a slug, or a green-spotted pig.

'Heinkel He III!' he shouted to Granda, proud of his knowledge.

The plane passed overhead. Every gun on the river was firing now. The pom-poms on the Bank Top, with their long evil black barrels, were spraying curves of shells you could actually see, because they left trails of smoke in the air. The Jerry actually flew into one curving spray. A mass of tiny fragments flew from its rounded wing tip and twinkled towards the earth, and Sonny gave a wild yell of glee; but the plane flew on, as if nothing had happened, and vanished round the bend of the river.

'I doubt we'll see him again,' said Granda. 'Like all greenhorns. He's the worm the early bird always gets.'

'What you mean?' asked Sonny.

'A law of nature. The old hands survive, and the young greenhorns cop it – them that don't know their arse from their elbow. It was the same in the trenches. Most new kids went very quick. If they lived a week, they usually lived a long time. They'd learnt to keep their heads down, and not do anythin' daft. It's the same with the young birds in the spring – the cats get them. Never see a cat get an old bird. Old bird keeps good watch an' sees the cat coming a mile off. Only time an old hand cops it, is when he gets too cocky or too tired. Like the Red Baron. He was the best old bird there ever was, but he got too cocky – or too tired mebbe.'

'Eeh, you daft old beggar – ye've got the Red Baron on the brain.' Nana's voice came from far above their heads. Looking up, he saw her silhouetted against the red sky. Wearing her flowered pinny and a tin hat, with two more tin hats in her hand. Granda had come home with them, three days ago. Scrounged in exchange for fish. For some reason, they'd been blue, with 'Police' in white letters across the front. But Granda had quickly painted them grey, like the soldiers' at the Castle . . .

'You shove these on,' she said, handing them down.

'Eeh, aren't women marvellous? In peacetime it's "Wear your muffler" and now it's "Wear your tin hat".'

'We should be down the cellar.'

'Gerraway, woman, we're as safe as houses down here. This is the best trench Aah've dug since Passchendaele. Aall it wants is a firing-step. Come doon. Come into my parlour, said the spider to the fly! There's nowt to be scared of, it's only a single Jerry, an' there's not much left of him.'

He gave Nana a hand, and she came down with a rush, saying she was too old for this kind of thing, and the damp soil would bring on her rheumatics . . .

'Haad yer whisht. He's coming back, Aah think.

Those gunners at Newcastle need to get their eyes chaaarked.'

The guns were getting louder and louder again. But Sonny felt very safe, crouched between Nana and Granda, with the great weight of tin hat on his head, and the grass at the edge of the hole tickling his nose and smelling sweet and of peacetime.

The Jerry plane was flying a little lower now, but somehow it looked ill. It flew slowly, with one wing down, and a thin trail of white smoke coming from an engine. Daylight was showing through small holes in the wings, and its tail was ragged. As they watched, another storm of curving smoky trails seemed to go right through it, and slowly its undercarriage descended.

'He's going to land,' whispered Nana. 'Land in the sea. Oh, those poor young fellers on board . . .'

But the plane began to trail out towards the lighthouses at the ends of the piers as if, wearily, it still longed for home. And then, despairing, as if the weariness was too much, it settled on the little waves, and vanished behind a wall of spray.

'Me binoculars!' shouted Granda, leaping from the trench like a ten-year-old. 'Where's me binoculars?'

He ran to the kitchen and grabbed them off the back door, and focused them wildly. Sonny, clinging to his arm, could see the plane again, floating on the waves. Little figures had climbed out on the wing. Four, in bright life jackets. Then they began hammering at the plane's body with something that flashed in the setting sun.

'There's one of their mates trapped inside,' said Granda. Then, 'One o' them's gettin' out a little boat.'

He twiddled the centre-wheel of the binoculars. 'They're inflating the boat. They don't want to get wet. That'll cool their courage for them.'

'Can I have a look!' shouted Sonny, and reluctantly Granda passed the glasses over, and Sonny had to refocus them all over again, the sea and sky jumping about like a mad thing.

But he saw the end. The two men still hammering and pulling away bits of fuselage. And then, the terrible thing, the wings of the bomber folding upwards like the covers of a book, and the tail too, and the men on the wing leaping for their lives into the water. And then suddenly, with the flash of a black wing tip cross, the plane was quite gone.

'Down to Davy Jones's Locker,' said Granda. 'Aye well, *his* troubles are over.'

A noise of a chugging diesel engine drifted up behind them. A big, grey, naval launch swept past, with three sailors standing behind the helmsman, with rifles held at the ready. It headed straight for the four airmen, who were now bobbing about in the boat they'd inflated.

The two boats moved together.

They're helping them on board,' said Granda. 'Two of them's hurt, one bad I think.'

Now the launch was coming back. It passed so close to their cliff that Sonny could see everything. The leaping jet of steaming water that pulsed from the stern; the shiny brass-and-wood spokes of the wheel, as the helmsman turned it, the varnished deck-planks gleaming in the late sun . . .

And the Germans, looking inhuman, like seals, in their close-fitting black leather helmets. One stood in the cockpit; the armed sailors had lit up a fag for him, as well as themselves. He was talking at the top of his voice, even laughing with them, in a wild way.

Two more lay entangled on the top of the long cabin, the one in the arms of the other, and as they passed, the hurt one screamed out in agony, like a rabbit in a snare.

And on the bow, quite alone, away from all the others, a long shape under a red blanket. His head covered up, and only his black leather flying-boots showing. So still . . .

And behind him, he heard his nana weeping.

Granda shuffled uncomfortably; he didn't seem to know what to do with his hands. 'Come on, hinny, it's not like you to take on like that.'

She glared at him, through her tears. Shouted,

'They were all some mother's sons. Some woman had the pain of bearing them . . .'

Then the all-clear went.

'*Dear Sonny,*

Well, the balloon has really gone up now. Jerry is after our convoys with Stukas, and sinking a lot of ships. We are flying every hour of daylight now. The Polish chap has got two, one certain, one probable. He's a real ace. And, you'll never believe this, but my bloke got one yesterday. Did a victory roll right over the airfield, which the CO tore a strip off him for, after. But he was so excited when he landed, I don't think he noticed. He put me in mind of you at Christmas, his face all shining. He didn't look more than about twelve years old.

I have made friends with the crew of a Boforsgun. Army lads, guarding the airfield. I went for a walk to stretch my legs after dinner and came across them, stuck in a little sandbagged emplacement just inside the perimeter fence. They gave me a mug of tea, as they were having a brew-up. They let me have a look at their gun. It uses quite big shells, but fires them nearly as fast as a machine gun. Swedish job – I reckon them Swedes know what they're doing.

There is talk of giving me a third stripe, as our sergeant in charge of our flight is having a lot of bother with ulcers. They think he may have to go into hospital for an op. It's the work. It's non-stop now. Seven in the morning till near midnight, patching the planes up. They need every one they can for the morning. Somehow I don't think they've got many to spare.

Give Nana and Granda a big kiss and a hug for me.

Your loving Dad. (Soon to be sergeant, acting unpaid haha)

'Is your Granda joining the Home Guard?' asked Jackie Robinson, squashing a yawn. The sky was sultry with low cloud, the classroom was stifling in spite of all the windows being open, and it was nearly the end of term. For the last week they'd brought in books and games from home, and helped the teacher sort out her cupboards, but now everything was just *boring*.

'He hasn't got time,' whispered Sonny. 'He's got *us* to defend, outside the defences. We can't expect no help from the Army. There's nothing between us and Hitler but the North Sea. But he's got an old shotgun and some cartridges, and lots of bottles of petrol. He's got old rags stuck down the necks of them, an' he'll set the rags alight and throw them at the Germans when they attack our house. He calls them "Molotov cocktails" because that's what the Finns threw at the Russian tanks.'

'You lucky dog,' said Jackie, his eyes widening to saucers. 'All we've got is the bread-knife an' the carving-knife. Me dad'll have the carving-knife and me mam the bread-knife. Like ol' Churchill says, take one with you when you go! Our dog can get quite nasty too. Isn't it dangerous, having all that petrol around, in case a bomb hits it?'

'It's in the old rabbit-hutch by the back door. Cor, it doesn't half pong of petrol.'

'Can I come and see? Give you two copies of the *Beano* . . .'

'I'll see,' said Sonny, very loudly, and at that point the siren went. There was a great scrabbling under desks for gas mask cases.

'Ey, what's that noise?' said Jackie. 'Like a kid running a stick along railings?'

Just at that moment Miss Matthews bawled for silence, and Sonny heard it quite clearly. And a lot else. Aircraft engines, roaring and whining and zooming like a lot of mad violins. Dozens of kids running dozens of sticks along dozens of railings . . .

'S'a dogfight!' shouted Jackie, and in a moment all the class rushed madly for the door. The first people tried to shelter in the doorway, but those coming behind pushed them right into the middle of the playground. Everybody stared at the sky, but there was nothing to be seen, just low, grey, woolly clouds.

'Heck, what a swizz!'

'Hurry across to the shelter, children!' called Miss Matthews, desperately.

But just at that moment, one engine, invisible above, screamed into a diving crescendo, a section of woolly, ragged cloud darkened, thickened and became a diving Spitfire.

'Oh, *no!*' groaned Jackie, clenching his hands, thinking the Spitfire was going to crash. But, as they watched, heart in mouth, it began to pull out of the dive and head straight for them. Its wings shadowed the playground, the RAF roundels, numbers on the body, the trails of black soot streaming back from the gunports in the wings. A whiff of burning petrol, a Guy Fawkes' smell, and it was gone, climbing, climbing back to the battle.

'Go on, mate!' shouted Jackie. 'Give them Hell!'

The Spitfire became a ghost, a shadow in the cloud, and vanished.

'See me after school, Robinson,' said the headmaster, emerging last, with his arms full of school records. 'I will not tolerate such language in my playground.'

'Can we stay an' watch, sir?' chorused the class. 'It's boring down the shelter. We can't see nothing.'

'Certainly not!' shouted the headmaster. 'Take cover, take cover.' He tried to gesture with his full arms, and all the school records escaped him and fell on to the concrete of the netball court.

Those boys were really hammering those railings now.

'Machine guns,' said Jackie knowledgeably, drifting reluctantly towards the shelter, still staring at the sky. 'I wonder where all the bullets are going. I could do with a few.'

Just then, the row of tall poplar trees that had shaded the playground since time immemorial suddenly seemed to jump in the air. Then the tops began to fall one after the other in a neat row, rustling to the concrete. The windows of the houses behind dissolved into fountains of glass.

'Run!' screamed the Head. 'Run!' He was still desperately scrabbling up school records.

Again the noise of engines became deafening. Two dark shadows passed, inside the clouds. Then some smoking object appeared, far out over the sea. It twisted and turned, and then vanished behind the rooftops.

'Get in!' roared the Head, and rammed children through the shelter door so they packed up like sardines.

'Was a Jerry,' said Jackie.

'How'd you know?'

'Had two engines.'

'*Blenheims* have two engines.'

'Sit down, sit down all of you while Miss Matthews calls the register, oh dear where is the school-dinners book . . .'

'We'll look for bullets soon as the all-clear goes,' said Sonny.

They'd hardly got through 'There'll Always Be an

England' and were starting on 'Wish Me Luck as You Wave Me Goodbye' when the all-clear did go.

School finished early, which was great.

'There's all little white stars on the pavement,' said Sonny. 'In rows.'

'Wossat?' squealed Jackie, diving into the dry soil under a privet hedge.

It looked like a little silver mushroom, about three-quarters of an inch across.

'What the Germans dropping them for?' Sonny, joining him, had found half a dozen more. 'They look too small to explode, don't they?'

'Fool! They're *bullets*, flattened by hitting the ground,' said Podger Armstrong, passing very quickly. 'I've got twenty already. Kids' stuff.'

As they were reaching the broad expanse of Front Street, Jackie said, 'What's that smell of burning? Somebody started a bonfire?'

But, looking up Front Street, inland, they saw the huge black smoke-clouds towering into the sky.

'The Docks,' said Jackie, awed. 'They've hit the Docks.'

'No they haven't. The Docks is that way. That's just houses up there.'

'Shall we go and see?'

'It's miles, I think,' said Jackie regretfully. 'And me mam gets worried about me, after an air-raid. Best go home.'

But Sonny picked up little mushrooms all the way down the pier-approach. By the time he got home, his pockets were bulging and starting to tear. Some dogfight.

He found Granda wrathfully watching the smoke-clouds, which were slowly getting less.

'Cowards,' he said. 'Bombing ordinary decent people. They just jettisoned their bombs anywhere, when the RAF lads hit them. Like they was shitting themselves.'

Four days later, Sonny was walking down the pier-approach with Granda's evening paper when he saw the little dog. It was a very middle-aged little dog, with a smooth pale-yellow coat, thick body, thin little legs and ears that pricked up and then changed their mind. It seemed to be waiting for Sonny, its large dark eyes fixed on his in some sort of appeal, and one front paw in the air.

Sonny liked dogs. In the old days, he'd always been nagging Dad to buy him one, but Dad had always said, 'We'll see,' in a tone of voice that meant 'no'.

Sonny crouched down, and offered his fingers for the dog to smell, the way you ought to. But the dog suddenly gave a sharp growl and streaked off through the gap in the barbed wire by the sentry box. One of the two sentries aimed a kick at it, as it passed, and his hobnailed boot caught its tail, making it yelp.

Sonny didn't know either of the sentries. He gave the one who had kicked the dog a hard look.

'Don't look at me like that,' said the sentry. 'Where you off to? Where's your identity card?' As soon as he saw Sonny had it, he waved it away without looking at it. He was that sort of man.

Sonny walked through, then turned back and said, 'What did you kick that dog for?'

'Gets on yer bloody nerves,' said the sentry. 'If I

had my way, I'd shoot it.' The other sentry nodded agreement.

'I think you're *cruel*,' said Sonny.

'Just you wait,' said the sentry. 'You'll see.'

Sonny walked on. The dog was waiting for him again, all anxious. Again, when he held his hand out, the dog snarled and streaked away. But he had seen it wasn't a stray. It had a worn black collar and a little medallion. It was the sort of dog you saw with old ladies, usually tubby with too many tit-bits. But as this one turned to run, he saw with surprise that all its ribs were showing under its coat, sticking out even. He thought it was *very hungry*. And it only ran for a few yards, before the run collapsed into a three-legged limp. And there was a bloody patch on its shoulder, and he thought he saw a glint of white bone.

'Here, boy,' he called over and over. But over and over it ran away, just as he was about to touch it. And from the way it was panting, he could see it was very dry.

He left it, and went into the kitchen when he got home. But when he looked back, it was there with its nose stuck longingly through the garden gate, and again staring at him yearningly. Somehow he knew it was in terrible trouble.

'Granda?' he called softly. 'Granda?' Granda was snoring gently in the kitchen rocker, his reading spectacles in his lap, and the wreck of the morning paper round his feet.

On Sonny's third call, Granda uttered a series of wild snorts, like a walrus coming up for air, or a buffalo about to charge, and opened his eyes.

'Wassat?'

'I wouldn't have disturbed you,' said Sonny politely, 'only I knew you weren't asleep. Just resting your eyes.'

'Oh, aye, just restin' me eyes.' Granda hated to be caught sleeping during the day, because Nana told him it was a sign of getting old. 'But what's all this "Granda-Granda" business? It's "Granda-Granda" so often, I dream it when I'm in bed. Why don't you pick on the Almighty for a change? They say he *never sleeps*!'

'Granda, there's a strange dog outside. At the gate; he keeps looking at me as if he wants help, but then he just runs away.'

'Aye,' said Granda. 'I've seen him. Sometimes he runs in circles for hours, just for the sake of running. Aah think his mind's gone . . . Aah think he must have been in the bombing. Aah've seen fellers like that, in the trenches in the Last Lot. Aall they were good for any more was eatin' and drinkin' and dodgin' shells. You couldn't get a word out of them, they'd never sit still for a minute. But somehow, they remembered about food an' drink an' shells.'

'What'll happen to it?'

'Probably run till it dies.'

Sonny was silent in horror. 'Can't we do anything? It's hurt as well.'

A strange smile, with a lot of sadness, came on to Granda's face. 'Eeh,' he said, 'you look so like your mam. Always worried about some lame duck, she was.'

Sonny saw an opening. 'If Mam had seen it, she'd have tried to help it . . .'

'Eeh, you know how to twist a feller's arm. Go an' get the enamel bowl from the sink, half-full of water then. But if ye take that dog on, Sonny, it's your responsibility. Once you give it stuff, you'll have to go on giving it stuff. Go an' put the bowl of water just inside the gate. But not where yer nana'll fall over it, when she comes home wi' the shoppin'.'

When Sonny had done so, he came back to the kitchen window, where Granda stood with his binoculars, watching the dog.

'If it won't come for the water, there's no hope for it. They might as well shoot it and put it out of its misery.'

They waited a long time. Through the glasses. Sonny could see the dog seemed to be in torment. He could see its nose working, as it sniffed the water. It put its head through the gate, one paw even; but it always drew back.

'Aye well,' said Granda, 'you tried. I've got things to do.' So, sadly, Sonny went with him, to feed the half-dozen hens in their cree round the back, and pull weeds from among the carrots. He could not get the poor lost dog out of his mind, but he just got on with things miserably. That was what you had to do in wartime.

He was roused from his misery by a shout from Nana.

'What's ma washing-up bowl doin' in the middle of the path. Aah nearly broke me neck . . .'

He looked. The bowl was empty.

'Did you empty the water out, Nana?'

'No, it was as dry as a bone.'

'Aye,' said Granda. 'Well, there's hope yet. That

water couldn't have evaporated by itself. It's not that warm a day. You can put out some more water in the morning . . .'

The next morning, the dog was waiting at the gate again. It ran off when Sonny put down the bowl, but the moment he went back into the house, it leapt on the wall, wriggled through the wire, and began to lap furiously, the water coming over the side of the bowl in waves.

'Aye well,' said Granda, 'it's not goin' to die o' thirst. But that's a nasty wound it's got. What you done wi' that beef-bone you got, Sarah?'

'That's to make a soup.'

'Aah'm sick o' soup. Give the bone to the bairn, for the dog. There's a few bits of meat on it . . .'

'What we goin' to live on then? Fresh air?'

'Aah'll nip down the Quay for a bit o' fish, after.'

'Well see you do!'

'Put the bone halfway down the garden path, Sonny. We'll make this lad work for his supper.'

It seemed cruel to Sonny, to put the dog through its agony again. The quivering, sniffing nose through the gate, the slow and painful crossing of the wire, the creep on its belly up the garden path, jumping at every tiny noise. But, finally, the dog snatched the bone and ran, and vanished.

'Ey,' said Granda next morning. 'We've got a new next-door neighbour.' He nodded towards the window, and Sonny looked out.

There was a place for the dustbins, beside the gate. A kind of stone table, under which the dustbins sat.

But this morning, something else sat there as well. From the dark cavern to the left of the bins, a small yellow prick-eared head looked out warily.

'He's found a home,' said Granda. 'A safe place. Aah couldn't ha' picked a better place meself, for when the bombs is droppin'. Wise beasts, dogs. And he can whip back out o' the gate, if we get too much for him.'

'Aah hate to think of the poor beast cowering there,' said Nana from the stove, where she was frying bread for breakfast. 'Stinkin' hole, an' all them flies. It'll catch some disease . . .'

'Gerraway, woman, first things first. Once in France I had to dive down a French lavatory when Aah heard a shell coming. A very full lavvy it was, an' all.'

'Lucky for you Aah didn't have to wash your clothes in them days. Fellers haven't got the sense they were born with. Babbies that need their noses wipin' from the cradle to the grave.'

'The trenches weren't no place for babbies.'

'*Murderous* babbies, the lot o' you. Men are always wantin' to kill something, and if there's nowt else they kill each other.'

'What shall we do with the dog next, Granda?' asked Sonny quickly, before a real argie-bargie started.

'There's some porridge-scrapings an' a bit of old stew,' said Nana. 'Mix them up an' give that to it.'

'Aye,' said Granda. 'Heat it up to give it a good smell, then put it on the doorstep. Make him come for it. It's the only way.'

It was a long time before the dog crept up to the

back door. Three times it bolted back to its safe refuge. The least noise seemed to terrify it, even the call of a seagull on the chimneys. But in the end, it was there, wolfing the food down, body twisting and turning, looking everywhere, ears cocked. Then it fled.

'Leave him bide,' said Granda. 'He's watching us, weighing up everything we do. He wants to join a pack. All dogs do, like wolves. He's wondering if we're the right pack to join. So just go about things as usual, ignore him, and leave him to make his own mind up.'

When Sonny went up for Granda's paper, the dog cowered deep into its new lair. All he could see were the two shining points that were its eyes, following him as he walked past. And there was a low growl, as he shut the gate.

But when he came back, the dog was running around the grass of the headland. Not aimlessly, blindly, but sniffing at posts and tufts of grass, and peeing a little on every one.

'Good sign,' said Granda. 'He's marking out his new territory, leaving his calling cards. He'll stay now.'

But it was not the dog waiting on the doorstep the following morning. It was a grey-and-white cat, just sitting there expectantly. The only thing was, it had not a whisker to its face, and all its fur was oddly frizzled down one side. And when Granda clapped his hands loudly near its head, it didn't even notice.

'Deaf as a post,' said Granda. 'Another one bombed out. Give it a saucer of milk, Sarah. They're copping it bad, up in the town now.'

Sonny, still yawning from a night down the cellar, remembered all the bumps and thumps of the night before. But they seemed just a dream . . . 'Can I go up and see the damage, Granda?'

'Mebbe. We'll give the Rescue gangs a chance to clear things up first. There's some things young bairns shouldn't see.'

'*Dear Sonny,*

Sorry about this scrawl in pencil. Our billet was flattened by a bomb yesterday; and the Naafi. The poor old place doesn't look much like home any more. I scrounged this pencil off a GPO man who was working to mend the telephone wires. He'll take out this letter and post it for me. I don't want the censor's blue pencil all over it.

Sad news, I'm afraid. My Polish chap has bought it. It was the worst day yet yesterday. More Jerries than wasps round a jam pot. The sky was black with them. The Polish feller hit a Jerry in the first wave, and knocked him down, but the Jerry set his plane on fire. He should have baled out, but the rest said he just seemed to go bonkers. He knocked down another Jerry and then rammed the leading plane in the next wave head-on. Still, that's the way to go, I suppose. Churchill said take one with you when you go; he took three. We won't forget him in a hurry. But we could do with him now. He was a good pilot, the best.

We are so short of pilots, my young bloke has been made a flight-commander, with two

103

blokes under him who look even younger. One of them told me he'd only had seventeen hours in Hurricanes. What can a young kid like that do?

We just work till all hours, getting the planes ready for the morning. Luckily Jerry doesn't come at night! Then we just curl up in the hangar under a blanket. One thing about being tired, you can certainly sleep anywhere.

Love to Granda and Nana. Be a good boy.
Your loving Dad.

They slept down the cellar every night now. It was warm and dry and safe, and saved getting out of bed if the siren went. Granda had scrounged a couple of the wooden bunks that were installed in every Anderson shelter. He slept himself in a huge, old armchair that had seen better days, but was saggy and comfy. Two hurricane lamps, hanging from the ceiling, threw a cosy, golden light over all the old familiar things. A row of drooping sacks contained the last of the winter vegetables, potatoes and turnips, shrivelled and rotting now, giving off a sweet-sour smell. But Nana still rummaged among them for something good enough for a stew, even though there were the new vegetables in the garden. Waste not, want not, she always said.

Jars containing eggs preserved in isinglass, rows of jars of bottled fruit and jam. And Nana's famous elderberry wine in its dark, dusty bottles. The newer bottles had garish balloons from Christmas popped over their open necks. Some, where the animal in the wine was still busy, were quite plump. Others, where the animal had gone quiet, were as shrivelled as the turnips. But there were older bottles, from 1939 and 1938 and even 1937. They didn't go rotten, just got stronger with the years. Nana had given the young curate from Holy Saviours a glass of her 1937, and it had tasted so nice he'd asked for another and got it, while a slow smile grew across Granda's face. It tasted so harmless; but the curate had fallen off his bike in Front Street and had had to be helped home, saying some very odd things about the nature of the Holy Trinity that had quite shocked the churchwardens. Nana's elderberry was *lethal* . . .

And there was Granda's work-bench, with the tools all oiled and hung in neat rows, and the great scythe on the wall, which he used to mow the grass of the headland . . .

All so . . . safe . . . so usual. And the cat, which had been waiting at the cellar door, the moment they started to get ready for bed and fill the hot-water bottles, was poised on the end of the work-bench, purring and rocking to itself.

Granda stirred, and cocked an ear.

'Siren.'

'Might be nowt,' murmured Nana, opening one eye, and making herself more comfortable.

'No,' said Granda. 'Here the beggars come.'

The engines grew loud, even down the cellar. Wild, lunging, coming and going.

'Lot o' them,' said Granda. 'Hitler really means it tonight.'

'Aah wish that beggar had died at birth,' said Nana. 'They shoulda drooned him, like an unwanted kitten.'

Now the guns opening up from the Castle. Tiny

tremors came through the ground, and up the legs of the bunks. Little bits of whitewash detached from the curving bricks overhead, and fluttered down through the lamplight, like little wobbling parachutes. The cat stirred his paws uneasily, as the vibrations of the work-bench reached them. It stopped purring, and its ears went down. They had called it Grimalkin.

'It *knaas*,' said Granda. 'Wise beast.'

Sonny worried about the dog, out there under the stone table in the garden. The bangs must be terrible for dogs; dogs heard things four times louder than human beings. Perhaps it would go out of its mind again, and start running in those aimless circles.

The ground shook harder; a shower of flecks of whitewash, near a twinkling blizzard.

'Bombs,' said Granda.

'Sou' Shields, mebbe,' said Nana. 'Aah hope they don't hit those oil-tanks.'

'Nearer than Sou' Shields, hinny. Up in the town.'

'Aah hope Cousin Millie's all right. Jack's on nights this week. She gets so scared. Frightened she'll get buried alive in that shelter.'

'She'll have to tek her chance, like the rest of us. Aah think Aah'll just nip up for a look-see . . .'

'You'll do nowt of the sort, ye daft old fool . . .'

Granda was just getting to his feet when the next bomb dropped, quite far off. But then there was another, nearer. And another nearer still. And a fourth. Like the footsteps of some monstrous giant, getting closer and closer.

'Eight to a string,' Sonny saw Granda mouth. Then Granda was counting. Five . . . six . . . seven . . . Then they heard the scream of the eighth. Louder,

louder. Granda said you never heard the one that got you, but how did he know? Sonny stared at the whitewashed brickwork, as if his life hung on it. It might be the last thing he ever saw ... Just when the screaming got unbearable, there was a wider, softer, duller thud.

'That one's in the sea, Aah'll bet,' said Granda, and started up the cellar steps. He opened the cellar door, then Sonny heard him open the kitchen door to the outside.

There was a wild skittering of claws, and then a small, furry bundle flew down the cellar steps and hurled itself into Sonny's arms, where it quivered and whimpered. It seemed to be trying to bury itself in Sonny's body, creep down inside Sonny's blankets. He stroked the pointed ears, flattened to the skull with terror. Spoke softly to it, reassuringly.

'Aah see you've got a new friend,' said Granda, coming back. 'A new member of the family. Well, it's an ill wind ... and that bomb *was* in the sea. Aah could still see the ripples. An' it's killed a lot o' fish. The sea's covered wi' them, all sorts. And they're coming in wi' the tide. The moment the all-clear goes, Sonny, we'll off and catch them. Afore the sun an' the sandflies get at them. There'll be a lot o' blackjack, but folk'll eat anything these days ...'

The all-clear had gone. To the west, towards Newcastle and nearer, the sky glowed bright pink. There was a great new bite out of the headland, beyond the garden wall.

'Number seven did that. And you can see number six further along, that big hole by the monument.

And number eight went into the sea the other side of us. We've been pretty lucky, Sonny! But if it hasn't got your number on it . . .'

Granda's hands were full of old straw fish-baskets. He led the way down the steps to the cove. There were quite high waves breaking on the shore, under the moon to the east. The sky in the west was pink and the sky to the east was blue-silver. And under the moon, every wave was full of shining silver fish.

'Anything bigger than a sardine,' said Granda, and began to stoop and fill the first basket. 'What people won't eat, they'll have for their cats . . . What you going to call your dog?'

'Blitz.'

10

Sonny sat on the steps of Collingwood's Monument, with Blitz at his feet. He had Blitz on a leash; the dog seemed to like it that way. He kept close to Sonny all the time now, even when he was in the house. Sonny could do no wrong in Blitz's eyes, though the dog still growled at Nana and Granda occasionally, when they made a sudden movement he wasn't used to.

Still, they had done a lot. Had Blitz to the vet. The white thing that had showed in the middle of his injured shoulder hadn't been bone; just a little piece of white plaster or something, embedded in the wound, which the vet had taken out. The wound was healing nicely now, a dried scab that would fall off in its own time, Granda said, and then the hair would grow again.

They had read the name and address on Blitz's collar, and Granda had gone to see the people. But he came back shaking his head. The house was bombed flat, a mere heap of rubble. And the bomb had scored a direct hit on the Anderson shelter in the back garden. Opened it up like a tin-opener, Granda said. And he added grimly,

'They won't be needing Blitz any more.'

'No relations?' asked Nana.

'Some farming people up Hexham way, they said. But they didn't know their name, even. They just came for the funeral and went home straight after, afore the sirens went. It's us or the dogs' home, an' the dogs' home's full of blitzed dogs. He'll do better wi' us.'

So Blitz had stayed, and learnt to eat boiled fish-heads, and grown a little fatter and a little livelier. For Sonny he would do remembered tricks, begging for bits of biscuit with one ear up and one ear down. Or roll over on his back and die for his country . . . Every so often, without warning, he would start shivering and making puddles on the carpet and have to be dragged from the room. But Granda said he was just a wounded soldier, and wonderful considering what he'd been through.

Sonny stroked him, enjoying the feel of his fur in the warm sunshine of the marvellous morning, with the river twinkling like a million diamonds, all the way across to the hazy oil-tanks over at South Shields. Then he got out Dad's latest letter.

It was a very dreadful letter, because it said nothing really. Just the address and date, and,

'Dear Sonny,
    Well, we're still here, just. My young man is in hospital – bullets through both his legs, and they reckon he'll never fly again. I expect he's glad to be out of it. One of the young kids is flight-commander now, I forget his name. The latest pilots have only had nine hours' practice in Hurricanes—'

And there the letter stopped. Without even a signature. And the envelope was all oily black fingerprints, and a stain that might have been beetroot or tomato or blood. And there was a sharp dent in it, as if something heavy had fallen on it, and when Sonny had opened it, a little stream of red, grating powder that might be brick dust had fallen out on to his trousers. It all said 'bombing' as clearly as Blitz's wound; the letter itself was a casualty.

Where would it all end? Sonny lay on his back and peered up. Above his head, the four great, black cannons from Admiral Collingwood's flagship still thrust their muzzles out to threaten the sea. And the Admiral, all bulging chest and chin from this position, still kept watch to seaward. But what could *he* do? He had won the Battle of Trafalgar once, as much as Nelson. But a quiet home-loving man, they said. A farmer with his own lands at Hexham. Not a man to make a fuss. He had said, just before the battle started, that he wished Nelson would stop making all those silly signal-messages . . .

What people didn't know was that Collingwood never came home from Trafalgar either. Nelson died with glory, the nation's darling. Collingwood stayed at sea, all those long years, keeping the French and Spaniards safely bottled up. Longing to feel dry land under his feet until he died of it. They sent him plants, to cure his homesickness, dogs even. But in that blistering salt-laden air, the plants and even the dogs died. Poor Cuddy Collingwood. Granda said they also served who only stand and wait . . .

He put away Dad's letter with a shiver. Well, Dad was still surviving. Four days ago, anyway. Hanging on. That was all you could do, hang on. And watch those newspapers which published the results of the

111

air battles of the south like cricket scores. A hundred and eighty-four Jerries down for thirty-four RAF. It looked like we were winning but . . .

He got up quickly, to shake off his mood. Walked down to the little beach of The Haven. Early that morning, from his lookout windows, he had watched a boy playing with his dog, swimming in the sea. He'd longed to rush down with Blitz and join in, it all looked so happy. But Blitz wasn't that kind of dog. The other dog, a black Alsatian, had looked a young fit lively dog . . .

Still, the boy might still be there now . . .

He was. But he was going. A roll of blankets on his back, tied by a leather strap. A small attaché case in one hand and the dog's leash in the other. Sonny thought he was a bit older than himself, a first or second year at secondary school. His face was pale and worried and tired. He didn't look like he was having much fun after all. He and Sonny nodded at each other, the two dogs moved closer, growling a little, then the older boy dragged his dog away, and up the pier-approach. Somehow, Sonny knew he was going . . . away. It made him sad. He would have liked to have known him.

FROM AIR MINISTY LONDON TO GEORGE
PRUDHOE ESQ. REGRET INFORM YOU YOUR
SON A/SGT PRUDHOE T 198753 KILLED IN
ACTION 26/8/40 LETTER FOLLOWS.
BARRETT J B WING COMMANDER.

The letter came three days later. Three days of silence in that house, when hardly a word was said, when people went about the tasks of seeing to the hens, cooking unwanted meals, clearing them away, washing up and just sitting, breathing and sighing occasionally. Nobody knew about the death but the three of them. They didn't want anybody to know, to sympathize, to come with flowers and whisper sadnesses. That was a burden for the weeks to come, when the news appeared, with Dad's photo in uniform, in the local paper. Now, they just wanted to sit together, and watch the patches of sunshine move across the floor and finally die away, and it would be time to draw the curtains and lock up and go and lie on their beds and hope to sleep, before another day of sitting and pain.

Granda opened the letter, with old trembling fingers, clumsily, so that Nana started up, saying, 'I'll get a knife.'

Granda read out loud, in a voice that grew slowly stronger:

> 'Dear Mr Prudhoe,
>   You will know by now that your son, Sergeant Thomas Prudhoe, was killed in action on the twenty-sixth of this month. He was a fine mechanic, a fine NCO much respected by those he led, and a popular figure in the squadron.'

Then Granda stopped, made a sound of disgust in his throat. 'He wouldn't ha' been popular. He didn't want to be popular. Why do they write such lies?' But his eyes were skimming on down the stiff paper of the letter. 'By God!' he said at last, and there was a different note in his voice. 'They're givin' him a medal for what he did.'

'What's he done?' cried Sonny.

Granda continued reading, with a rising excitement.

> 'His death in action occurred during a raid by German bombers on this airfield. A Bofors-gun had been put out of action by enemy machine gun fire, and one of its crew killed. Your son came on the scene, rallied the remaining soldiers, took over the aiming of the gun, and continued to fire at the enemy even after he had been wounded. Several hits on the enemy planes were observed, made by his gun among others, and one enemy plane was destroyed by an explosion in mid-air. Your son continued to fire the gun until the raid ended, in spite of serious loss of blood, finally dying in action. It is the opinion of all that his courage deserves recognition and your son has been recommended for the Empire Gallantry Medal by the Commanding Officer.
>
> I know how sad a loss this must be to you and your wife, and all here join me in sending their sincere condolences. I hope that the memory of your son's valour will do a little to ease the pain of your loss.
>
> We shall not forget him.
>
> B. E. Marsden, (Flt Lieut and Adjutant)'

There was a silence. And then Granda said, in a voice choked with grief and savage satisfaction,

114

'Well, by God, he took one with him.' And then the tears began rolling down his craggy cheeks. And in between, in that choked voice, he said things suddenly, out of the silence.

'Aye, he was a good shot – none better. He had an eye for it, even when he was a little lad.' Then, later,

'Dead with honour, Sonny – like *you* wanted. Well, he's got his glory now, and nobody can take that away from him.'

And later still,

'It was what he wanted. He never wanted to go on living, once your Mam was gone. He was like a fish out of water . . .'

And, finally:

'Aye well, we can hold our heads up. He ran a straight race, and he's in a better place now. Yer Mam'll have been waitin' for him. Nothing'll ever part them now.' He got up and said, 'Some fellers get a lot of grief from their sons. They turn into drunks, or go wi' other women, or thieve an' get sent to prison. Poor George Murphy, his son deserted, and was knocked down by a motor car, running away from the Military Police. Aah thank God your dad never ran away in his life. He's left me something Aah can be proud of.'

Then he went and got shaved, for the first time in three days, and put on his best suit, and took his silver-headed stick, which he hardly ever carried, and said, 'Aah'll go down to have a word wi' the fellers on the Quay. Aah'll not be long, Sarah. You and Sonny look after each other, till Aah come back.'

Nana went to the window, and watched him go, a long time. She said, softly, 'Aah thowt it would be the death of him, but Aah think he'll be all right now.' Then she said, 'Aah think Aah'll have a little lie doon. Ye'll be all right wi' yer dog, for a bit?'

'Yes, Nana.'

He went on stroking Blitz, who cuddled close to him, and thought how the world had changed. Heaven seemed very close, somehow; the door into Heaven had just closed behind Dad, or perhaps was still ajar.

11

Sonny stood very still, and very close to Granda and Nana both. His mind was already too full of too many things to cope with. The invitation to Dad's memorial service, from the RAF. The flurry of getting ready, that took two whole days. Leaving Blitz with Nana's friend, Mrs Meggitt. Leaving Grimalkin alone to guard the Old Coastguard Station, with plenty of water and a whole boiled fish-head outside the back door. Grimalkin watching, inscrutable, from the top of his favourite post, as the taxi drew away.

Being in their best clothes, with a suitcase. It was weirdly like going away on holiday, in the old days. The trains were packed, as they always were on Bank Holiday Monday; but now they were packed with soldiers, who lay about in their braces with their shirts undone and their caps off, and drank beer from the necks of bottles bought in a yelling rush at the stations.

Gliding into London, past the backs of tall burnt-out houses, and other houses cut in half, still showing wash-hand basins and pictures attached to walls five floors up where nobody would ever see or use them again. The taxi-driver taking them across London, because you couldn't move down the Tube for families who lived there all day long.

'Is there an air-raid on?' asked Nana, a bit nervously.

'Nah!' said the taxi-driver, in tones of great scorn. 'They don't dare come here any more by daylight, the sneaking bastards. Not since the fifteenth of September. That was a day, we was all outside cheering. The RAF caught them over London an' cut them to ribbons. Still get a few Jerry fighter-bombers, but they just drop their bombs on Kent an' scarper.' Then he added with a shudder, 'Now nights, they're a different matter! Whatever you do, be clear o' London afore dark!'

And then the great tall column of Nelson's monument in Trafalgar Square. Just that morning, he had said goodbye to Admiral Collingwood, when he took Blitz for his morning walk before Mrs Meggitt's. And now here was Admiral Nelson as well . . . It gave the whole world a magic strangeness, as if all the rules were different, and anything might happen at any moment, and it wouldn't worry you because you had nothing left to worry with, just this cool greyness in your head.

Then the little train, through the leafy countryside of Kent, fuller of trees than Northumberland could ever be. Those funny, pointed red roofs with sticky-out bits on top that Granda said were oast-houses. The cows and the sheep . . .

Granda had stirred, and stretched, in his best navy-blue overcoat, with all his medals pinned on the left breast.

'This is the way we came in 1915,' he said, sadly but dreamily. 'I swear it's the same railway line.

Nowt's changed at all. Twenty-five year and nowt's changed.'

'Except a lot of good fellers is dead,' said Nana, 'an' their wives scrimpin' as widows.'

'Aye,' said Granda. 'Aye.' He was very far away, looking out of the window. Sonny wondered what he was really thinking. He wondered if he himself would be on this line in twenty-five years' time, going to another war.

The RAF had met them at the station with a big blue bus and a blue officer inside. Not just Sonny and Nana and Granda but suddenly what seemed a hundred people getting off the train, who all looked the same. Dressed in their best dark clothes, stoop-shouldered and crushed, or heads back and so proud it hurt to look at them, like Granda. More than Dad had died. Many more. On the bus, a woman near the back began to cry hysterically. Granda bristled.

'She wants to get a hold on herself. Making an exhibition of herself like that.'

'Nana cries,' whispered Sonny.

'Aye, but she cries in private. Not where half the world can see her. This is not our day. It's to do honour to those who gave their lives that others might live. Greater love hath no man than this; that he lay down his life for his friends.'

By the time they reached the churchyard, the woman had shut up, or been shut up by her relations. It was a very leafy green churchyard, with a very old grey church, with walls full of flints. They straggled through the lychgate, past tombstones tangled in briars, with dates like 1856 and even 1789. Slowly the dates got later.

'A dearly beloved daughter, born April 4th 1929, died aged eight, September 7th 1937', 'Much Missed' and 'With God, which is much better.'

Nearly his own birthday. He wondered what she must have died of. Diphtheria, maybe? Or scarlet fever? Well, she'd missed the War . . .

And then, just a flat green stretch of turf, and the rows of long mounds of whitish chalky earth. Somebody had made little markers for each grave, just of white cardboard. It had rained a little, and they were crumpling and dribbling. He waited beside Nana, while Granda went off stiff-backed to find Dad. Dad's mound just looked like all the rest. A few little bits of grass and tiny weeds already pushed up through the soil.

Sonny stared at the mound, then told himself Dad wasn't really there, but with Mam in Heaven. He didn't think Dad would have liked this place very much, because it was so quiet and in the country and there were some bored cows shoving their heads over the churchyard wall, and chewing the cud noisily, with streams of spit drooling from their mouths, almost on to the graves. Even for holidays, Dad had never liked the country. He preferred the seaside, where there was a bit of life.

'Aye well,' said Granda. 'He's among his mates.'

'Mates?' whispered Nana, very shocked. 'There's a young slip of a lass buried next to him. Corporal Martha Strong aged twenty. Eh, bits of young lasses! It beggars belief!'

'WAAF,' said Granda, very much shaken, because he wiggled his moustache.

Sonny wondered, a little worried, if Dad and

Corporal Martha Strong had died at the same time, in the same raid. Would they have arrived in Heaven together? What would Mam have to say about that? She'd always been a bit sharp, when she accused Dad of giving some girl the eye . . .

'If you will return to the bus when you're ready,' called the officer, softly and gently. 'Lunch will be served in the sergeants' mess before the memorial service.'

It had been a good lunch, for wartime. Granda said as much; though he didn't eat a lot of salad, the ham was home-cooked and tasty. Sonny had eaten too much, which wasn't usual for him, but he sort of felt he needed to make himself more solid inside. Nana had got herself sat next to the parents of Corporal Martha Strong by some act of mysterious female magic, and had established that they came from Gateshead and were a very respectable family, the father being a plumber by trade, with his own business. Corporal Martha Strong had been going to be a teacher after the War. This seemed to cheer Nana up a little; it was almost as if Dad had been going to marry Corporal Martha Strong, rather than just be buried next to her . . .

But now they were standing out on the parade ground, all of them, in a hollow square; relatives on one side, and RAF men in well-pressed uniforms and WAAFs on the other three sides. The officers were there, wearing leather gloves, and the padre, looking odd with blue RAF trousers showing under his surplice, and a stole with an RAF crest blowing in the breeze from round his neck. And there was a man with a brightly polished bugle, and three men with rifles stood to attention. And a little RAF band.

The padre opened with prayers, which the wind blew away. They sang a ragged hymn, which was drowned by the band. Then the padre preached about patriotism, and men laying down their lives for their friends. Sonny didn't listen much. He was more fascinated by the wrecks of the huge hangars, still sticking up into the air like burnt rotten teeth. The great holes everywhere, filled up with rough, crushed brick and earth, even on the runway itself. And far off, in the dispersals at the far side of the runway, some mechanics were mucking about starting up the coughing engine of a stray Hurricane.

And then, it suddenly came real. The padre declaimed in a great voice,

'At the going down of the sun, and in the morning, we will remember them.'

And the riflemen came to life with a crash of metal, and raised their rifles high in the air, and fired three shots, all together beautifully, and there was that Guy Fawkes' smell again. And then the bugler raised his bugle to his lips, and sounded the Last Post. And then, after a silence, the reveille. And as the last note died, there came the sound of many engines, British engines, Merlins. And they came roaring in over the airfield in arrowheads of arrowheads, hardly above ground level. More Spitfires and Hurricanes than Sonny ever imagined could be in one place at one time. There might even have been a few Bolton Paul Defiants, though by that time Sonny's eyes were blurred with tears. Tears because they had won and were here to prove it, where no Jerry would ever dare to fly again. And Dad was part of it for ever now. They were flying on, free, and they somehow were taking Dad with them, back up into the sky. And in the thunder of many engines, it was suddenly all right.

'Aah feel better after that,' said Granda. 'They showed him . . . respect. They made me feel . . . he mattered.'

When it was finally all over, and the CO was shaking hands with every relative, he shook Granda's hand especially warmly, eyeing his medals.

'You were in the Last Lot, Mr Prudhoe?'

'Aye. In the trenches. Four years.'

'So was my own father. Though he wasn't so . . . lucky. Killed in 1917 . . .' Then the CO seemed to get a bit bothered, about having said Granda was lucky. He shuffled and said, 'If there's ever anything I can do . . .'

'Aye, there is,' said Granda. 'I want to see where my lad died.'

Again, the CO shuffled embarrassedly. Then he said, 'Well, I don't see why not, if you really want to . . .'

'Aye,' said Granda, fierce as anything, every inch the old soldier.

'Aah'll wait for ye in the bus,' said Nana. 'What about you, Sonny?' She eyed him, worried.

'I'll go with Granda.'

The CO pointed out where the Bofors-gun was and they walked, it seemed for ever, round the perimeter track. But it was easy to keep heading for the gun. Its long, thin barrel was still sticking in the air. Finally, they approached. There were some soldiers lounging about in a little hut near by, playing cards. The soldiers watched them curiously, but made no move towards either them or the gun. They walked right up to it.

Now Sonny could see the wounds that the Jerry machine guns had left. Long lines of gashes in the earth, that the grass had not yet grown enough to heal. Gashes heading straight for the gun. Where the gashes met the emplacement of sandbags, some of the older, greyer, bleached bags had burst, dropping little rain-blunted pyramids of white sand on the grass. Newer, bright brown sandbags, still stinking of creosote, had been laid on top. And the gun . . . big dents in the gun-mounting, daubed over roughly with red lead and green paint. Granda reached over and touched the gun, as if it was some beloved child . . .

'Sir, sir?' One soldier was hurrying across, anxious-faced. 'Sir, are you Sergeant Prudhoe's dad?'

'Aye!'

'I was with him, sir. That day I was his loader. I was the only one who survived. All the rest . . . bought it.'

Granda held out his hand. 'Put it there, son.'

'Gunner Umpleby's my name, sir. Royal Artillery. Sir . . . he was marvellous. After Smithy was killed, we all ran away. He shamed us. He got us back. Sir, he was a marvellous shot. He missed the first wave, through not quite having got the hang of the gun. But he hit a plane in the second – knocked the tip of its wing off. He got better all the time after that. He hit one in the third wave – in the port engine. I doubt it got home on one engine. But in the last wave – he got one right in the fuselage – it blew up. It blinded us.'

124

'There must have been other guns firin',' said Granda, very anxious to be fair.

'There weren't!' said Gunner Umpleby fiercely. 'They'd all run away. It was terrible – the Jerry air gunners were going for all our ack-ack guns. The only gun I could hear firing was ours. And then they hit him. But he went on firing. Till he just sagged, and died. Here, on this very seat. I tried to do what I could but ...'

Sonny stared at the seat. He stared at the circular gunsight, with its cross-hairs at the trigger of the gun, thick and curved with all the paint worn away so it was shiny ... These were Dad's last things, the last things he had seen ...

'Don't touch, son,' said Gunner Umpleby. 'It's loaded still. Though the beggars have never been back since ... that day. He saw off the last of them.'

They walked away; because the bus-driver had started up his engine, and was driving round the perimeter track towards them, and the officer was hanging anxiously out of the bus door.

Still Gunner Umpleby accompanied them. He shook hands a last time.

'You'll never know what he did, sir. There were some RAF blokes so scared by that time, they wouldn't come out of the shelters at all. Even when there was no air-raid on.'

'Aye,' said Granda, 'I know. We had some of that in the Last Lot too.' And he detached Gunner Umpleby's hand firmly but gently, and they walked up to the bus, where Nana was all in a fret waiting for them, wanting to get to the pub where they were going to spend the night.

12

They were still in London when dusk fell, the following evening. It was unbelievable; they'd had all day to get clear; but here they were.

The pub landlord had let them have a lie-in, after a night spent down the pub cellars among the reeking barrels of beer. Listening to the endless streams of bombers heading for London; nipping upstairs in the quiet times to watch the sky to the west, a pulsing living thing, pink and orange. They listened to the distant constant rumble of bombs, and the nearer bangs of the ack-ack guns. There was even a cool breeze, blowing off the sea, that the pub landlord said was on its way to fan the furnace that was London. In London there were fires so great they drew in oxygen from fifty miles away. The landlord's family talked a lot; nervously. About their relations in London, and the King and Mr Churchill, and whether they were still alive. They said if this went on much longer, there'd be nothing left of London. And they talked about when the Germans came, the Panzers roaring and crunching up their little country road, tearing apart the hedgerows. Their bags were packed . . . In all this, the bombing of Sonny's home town seemed very small, a mere sideshow.

The people even feared that British night-fighters might strike back at the bombers, for when they were attacked, Jerries just dropped their bombs anywhere, on the open countryside; a little church had been demolished only five miles away.

To make up for their lack of bed, the landlord had laid on a huge breakfast. Porridge and bacon and egg, thick rashers. Whatever they were suffering from, in this rich countryside, it was not short rations. New-laid eggs, with the straw still on them; rashers cut from a whole side of bacon that hung in the cool stone pantry.

Eventually, about midday, they set off to walk the two miles to the station. It was hot and sultry, and the green roads were tricky without signposts, removed in case German paratroopers landed and used them to find their way. They got lost several times. Granda found the suitcase hard work, and often paused to rest, pretending to admire the green, lush countryside. Kent, he said, was called the Garden of England. There were apples and pears dangling invitingly from trees. There were apples and plums for sale, at roadside tables, so lovely that Nana acquired two carrier bags full; and was able to buy some eggs too and a fresh young rabbit. Soon she was as laden as Granda. And everyone they met seemed to want to talk about the coming Invasion and . . .

The result was that they missed the two o'clock train. And the three o'clock was held up by signal failure near Headcorn Station. And then there was the struggle through the London Tube, with the platforms clogged by people who had already booked their sleeping places for the night, and were stretched out on the platforms, coming to within a yard of the edge, so that real travellers were in danger of being pushed on to the line as the train came in. They got lost on the Tube system too . . . and Nana's big bag of plums got squashed and started to leak juice.

Now they sat on the six o'clock from King's Cross to Newcastle. Which had already been delayed half an hour by a blocked line.

'Be at least another quarter-hour getting going,' said a friendly porter. 'That's if the siren doesn't go. If it does, you'll have to get off and go down the shelter. Could be till morning. Trains don't run in air-raids, too good a target.'

Granda had gone off to the buffet, to try to get something apart from apples and squashed plums, which Sonny had eaten too many of already, so that he felt like going to the toilet, only you couldn't while the train was in the station . . .

'He's been gone ten minutes,' said Nana, very worried, consulting the old pin-on watch on her frock. 'He's cutting it fine. Trust him.'

Just at that point, the train began to thrum; there were hisses high up in the roof. The train moved violently a yard, backwards.

'Oh, it's going!' wailed Nana. 'I knew he shouldn't have gone.' She stuck her head out of the open window, anxiously looking for him.

The train gave another jerk, and the station, the people, the porters, trolleys full of parcels began to slide away.

'George! GEORGE! George *Prudhoe*!' screeched Nana, as if she was afraid every George in London might come suddenly running to her aid.

And then, faintly, in the distance, the sirens went. Sonny no longer knew what to hope for. He simply prayed a general call for help. But no help came. The train quickened its pace, as if in response to soft explosions sounding from behind, and soon they were gliding quite swiftly through the darkness.

'Oh, yer Granda's back in that lot. And he's got our rail-tickets in his pocket an' all. What we goin' to do? What we goin' to tell the ticket collector at Newcastle? An' those perishin' Jerries'll kill him for sure . . .'

It was the last straw. Now even the remnants of their little family was broken up and disaster would come pouring in. It felt like the end. Nana turned a desperate face to him, and tears were glinting in her indomitable eyes. Was there no end to the cruelty of war? How would they cope without even Granda?

The carriage door slid open. Nana whirled with an appeal to the ticket collector . . .

But it was Granda standing there, grinning from ear to ear, as if he'd done something wonderful. And he had. There were sandwiches in his hands, and pork pies and Smith's crisps, and even what looked like a copy of the *Wizard*. And from each pocket of his coat protruded the neck of a bottle. Tizer on the left, and brown ale on the right. It was a feast; he might have been Santa Claus. But above all, he was here. Not lying like a bloody rag in some bomb-blast.

'You stupid old beggar!' roared Nana. 'You had me worried sick. You oughta have more sense, your age. Where you been?'

'Nipped aboard the train lower down. You weren't worried about *me*, were you? Aah'm the proverbial bad penny. Aah always turn up.'

'You silly old fool! You nigh gave me a heart attack! Don't you stand there grinnin' like the Cheshire Cat!'

She looked so angry; she sounded so angry. But the more angry she got, the more Granda just grinned at her, like a great big kid, pleased as Punch with himself.

People were *funny*, Sonny thought. Why wasn't Nana gladder? Why wasn't Granda sorrier? But he just asked,

'Have you got me a *Wizard*?' to restore law and order.

'Then the sirens went,' said Nana, a bit quieter. 'If they stop the train, we'll have to go down some shelter. If there's room . . .'

They sat and kept the lights off, all but the little dim blue light that burnt in the ceiling. They watched, as behind them in the city, the searchlights came on, one after the other, until the whole sky seemed cut into a jumbled tartan pattern of light from their blue swinging beams. How could any bomber escape from them? There was a series of flashes, like lightning, behind the sharp silhouettes of the north London terraces. Distant heavy rumbles like thunder, beneath the sounds of the train wheels. They held their breath and watched and listened, as London's agony grew behind them, and once again the sky assumed that pulsing pink and orange. The train slowed almost to a standstill several times, making Sonny go back to his desperate prayers, but always his prayers seemed to be answered, and the train picked up speed again, to the frantic chuffing of the engine. Finally, as they passed through a dim little station, they saw a local

130

train drawing up on the other platform, and heard a porter shout,

'Potter's Bar!'

'We're clear,' said Granda, with a long-exhaled sigh. 'Aah nivvor heard the Jerries were bombin' Potter's Bar.' And he relaxed and unscrewed the stopper of the bottle of brown ale.

'Aah don't know how you can drink that stuff,' said Nana, pulling a face, still not entirely ready to give up the quarrel.

'Have a sup,' said Granda, offering her first swig from the bottle. She pushed it away vigorously, and then suddenly she was laughing at his comical expression, and the quarrel was over.

And suddenly, Sonny felt . . . saved. Whatever sent down death from the sky had had mercy on them tonight, was suddenly somehow on their side. Mam had died, and then Dad had died, but now there was an end to dying. After this, he knew they would go on, the three of them. Till they died safe in their beds, in their own good time, as Nana would have said. He looked at Granda, over the edge of his comic and said,

'How old are you, Granda?'

'Me? Aah'm fifty-nine next birthday. Why'd you want to know?'

Sonny was too embarrassed to say. But Granda seemed to twig what he was up to.

'Plenty of life in the old dog yet. Me old father was hale and hearty till he was eighty-five. Dropped down dead sudden tryin' to carry six fish-crates at once. Hadn't been for them fish-crates, Aah swear he'd be with us yet. Don't worry, Sonny, Aah'll be there to drink your health on your twenty-first birthday. Aah'll probably be there to help you drink up your old-age pension. And yer Nana's even better – only fifty-six. You'll not be left alone in a cruel, hard world.'

And suddenly, they *were* a little family. The gap of the missing healed over. It still hurt; but this was a family that worked again; the future came back, like the dove to the Ark.

Sonny settled, content to be sad, to read the *Wizard* and chew his way through an old dry and stiff meat pie. The guard was coming down the train, shouting 'Blackouts, please' as well as 'Tickets, please'. Granda pulled down the blackouts on their rollers, and switched on the little, glowing, green light above Sonny's head. It was nearly as cosy as being at home. Nana had produced her knitting from the leather shopping bag she always carried with her, the one made of little patches sewn together. Her needles clicked a soft echo of the train's wheels over the lines. 'We're going-home, we're going-home,' the wheels seemed to say.

They didn't get back home till gone eleven. Luckily, there was no air-raid in the north that night, and Granda blew his last coppers on a taxi, so they arrived in style.

The first thing Sonny noticed, by the light of Granda's little torch as he opened the front door, was that there were no longer three sets of wellies in the little porch. The middle pair, Dad's, was gone.

'Aah gave them to a feller down the Quay,' said Granda softly. 'Poor Manny Josephs, he hadn't a pair to bless himself with, and his feet were gettin' soakin'.

132

Aah thowt you wouldn't mind, Sonny. Aah don't hold wi' keepin' relics. Aah've got more to remember yer Dad by than a pair of old wellies.'

Sonny nodded. Somehow, it was another step on the journey.

13

They were lifting the last of the garden vegetables. The huge main-crop potatoes; the swedes before the first frosts got to them and turned them sweet and nasty. It was a fine, frail evening again, October had come, and Sonny was back at school, where he was not only a hero now, but a hero's son too. Dad's posthumous medal had been announced, and the *Evening News* had turned it, Granda said, into something more heroic than Rourke's Drift. Sonny didn't much like being a hero's son; people were very respectful, almost as if he was the King or something; but they didn't come too close, and it made him feel both grand and lonely. Other people might get the cane, for misbehaving, but somehow he knew he never would ... It seemed vaguely wrong, as if he was excused life altogether ...

Blitz was with them, yapping excitedly every time they unearthed yet another huge cluster of potatoes, shoving his nose into the damp soil and sneezing. Grimalkin, as ever, watched in his dignified way from the top of his favourite post. There was a drifter, sailing out to sea, tooting urgently from the river below. Granda straightened over his shovel, put his hand to his back as if to make sure it was still there, and waved vigorously.

'Billie Hughes, in the *Min and Bill*. That Jerry had

a go at him, while his nets were down, Tuesday night. But Jerry got more than he bargained for. Billie's got two pairs of Lewis guns on his bridge now, and none of them jammed, for once. Jerry got sick of it first. Trawler's made of steel plates half an inch thick. Jerry planes are just aluminium like our kettle. Went off trailing smoke . . .'

'The Flying Pencil?'

'Aye, one of the old sort, he said.'

So the Jerry was still around. Dad was gone, and the Jerry was still around. God was being mocked. All Dad's efforts, all Dad's guts . . . But they'd been told the plane Dad knocked down was a Junkers 88 . . . A terrible dark cloud descended on Sonny's mind, a cloud so grey and swelling and terrible that he had to speak or die.

'It was my fault really. Mam *and* Dad. If I hadn't forgotten that box of matches, they'd both still be at home now. It was *me* that did it!'

Granda heard him out, not looking at him, picking up a bit of stick and using it to clean his shovel till the bare metal shone like silver. Then Granda let him cry. Not cuddling him, as Nana would have done, but standing beside him with his big hand on his shoulder, squeezing tight, as they both stared out to sea, though Sonny could see nothing but blurred blue light through welling waves of tears. It was better than cuddling; it was free, and the grief was not shut in, it went away, out over the sea.

Finally, when Sonny had fallen silent, apart from a few gulps, Granda said, 'Aah killed a feller that way, once. He was my best mate. On the Ancre in 1918, when we were startin' to win. Willie Robling was his name. We'd been through nigh four years of war together. You want to hear about it?'

'Yes.'

'Well, it was an evening very like this; peaceful. Jerry was in a bad way by that time. Didn't even shell us any more unless some fool provoked him. Short of shells they were, an' their guns so worn out that what shells they had used to land on their own men in the trenches. We were gettin' ready for the last Big Push, across the Hindenburg Line, Jerry's last defence. Sunny, it was; the lads had their shirts off, tryin' to get a bit of a tan. And we were in a set of fresh trenches that Jerry had kindly left for us, so they even smelled sweet. Plenty to eat, too. Seemed like Paradise, apart from the lice in your shirt. There was wild flowers, growing just beyond the parapet, and the birds was singing. Bet you didn't know we had birds, even there . . . ?'

'No.'

'Anyway, Willie and I were sitting together, on the firing-step, Willie just smokin' his old pipe and me writin' to yer nana, and we could even hear the Germans in their trenches, across no man's land, jabbering away in their own lingo. Then up comes the company sergeant-major. Adjutant wants a message running back to Brigade. Nowt important, just a ration-return for the following day. But he says you take it, pronto, Corporal Prudhoe. He never had much love for me, that sergeant-major; couldn't bear to see me happy or idle.

' "Oh hell," I says. "I wanted to finish this letter to the wife, afore I went on sentry."

' "I'll go for you, Geordie," says Willie, getting up

136

and grabbing the message off the sergeant-major. Afore he could argue, Willie was gone.

'Aah never saw him again. There was a new German sniper we didn't knaa aboot, lying ready wi' his rifle lined up on a bit of trench where the sandbags weren't quite together enough. Got Willie wi' his first shot. Don't knaa why the Jerry was so keen – they'd lost the War by then, an' they knew it. Didn't do him any good, either. Some of the lads got together, and held up an old helmet at the place where Willie had copped it. Jerry fired again – we were on to him, and he didn't live to see the morning.

'Aall through the War in the trenches, with never a scratch, old Willie. An' then he cops it, wi' four months to go. An' if I'd gone wi' that ration-return, it would ha' been me instead of him. An' he left a wife an' five little kids. Aah felt terrible, because yer nana only had yer dad to fetch up.'

'Did you ever . . . go and say sorry?'

'Aye, on me next leave . . . after the Armistice. Aah'd nivvor have had any peace o' mind, else.'

'What did she say?'

'She thanked me for telling her. But she didn't seem aall that bothered. Eight months had passed, and there was a new feller hanging aboot, getting in her coals an' mendin' her kitchen window, like. Just bein' helpful to the widow, but Aah could see what he was after. Alf Meggitt, it was. An' him a dried-out old stick of a bachelor, nigh fifty, that nobody ever thought would marry. But Aah don't blame him. She was a fine figure of a woman, in spite of having five kids. An' he was a good husband to her, and a good

137

father to her kids, though they never had none of their own—'

'Mrs *Meggitt*? The lady who looked after Blitz? *Nana's friend?*'

'Aye. What's got you so pussy-struck about *that*?'

'She always looks so cheerful . . .'

'Bless you, son, that was more than twenty year ago. The quick cannit live by the dead. Ye cannit grieve for ever. Who could bear it? Though some women did. Ye can still pick them out by their black widow's weeds. Wastin' their life, mekkin' other people miserable.'

Sonny was lost in awe, that life should heal over so. But then trees healed over; though you could still see where they'd lost a branch, years ago. The grass grew, where a Jerry bomber had crashed and blown up. He remembered the little weeds growing on Dad's grave. But it seemed more awful than good, that life should heal; as if people had never existed. He said stubbornly,

'It was still my fault. Mam and Dad.'

'Son!' Granda knelt beside him, his faded blue eyes very earnest. 'Ye cannit take the blame for yer Dad. Aah should be the last to say it, but yer Dad wasn't a very good dad to you. Another sort o' dad would ha' stayed home and stuck it out in that lonely house, an' takken care o' you. That was his *duty*! How would he have managed if he hadn't had yer nana an' me? He couldn't ha' gone tearin' off then. An' he would be alive today. There, Aah've said it. Yer dad wasn't scared o' Jerries, or o' dyin' but he was dead scared o' loneliness. No man's a hero all roond the houses.'

'But *Mam* was my fault . . .'

'Look, Sonny, it sometimes seems to me that that Great Feller Up There in the Sky, he sets traps for people, an' they walk straight into them, like unsuspecting mice. A mouse doesn't mean to get caught, he just wants a nice bit o' cheese. But bang goes the door o' the trap, an' he's caught for good an' he's got to live wi' it. That comic, that *Wizard* you wanted to read so bad, that night, that was your bit o' cheese. An' yer mam lovin' you, that was her bit o' cheese. An' that Jerry, that was yer dad's bit o' cheese. So ye're inside yer trap now, and there's nowt you can do about it, except keepin' on livin'. An' mek the most of yer mana and me, till we snaffle up our bits o' cheese. Right? Aah can only promise that Aah'm a fairly wily old mouse by this time an' so is yer nana, an' we'll tek a fair bit o' catchin'. So let's get on an' finish this patch o' taters.'

Sonny bent his back to his work again, thinking hard about mousetraps and cheese. It seemed to fit, to help, more than what the vicar had said.

Mam came to him in his dream that night, and smiled at him. She was still wearing her headscarf and carrying two shopping bags.

'You don't still do shopping?' he asked her.

'Oh, we're very busy up here . . .'

'Have you seen me dad?'

'Aah've seen him. He's all right.'

'Why didn't you fetch him?'

'They're having a bit of a job wi' him. He's too angry at the moment. He won't let go.' She frowned a little; her forehead showing its three rows of creases, the way it always had.

'Angry about that Jerry?'

'Aye, about that Jerry.'

'Tell him . . . I'll do what I can.'

She frowned again. 'Don't you worry about that Jerry. You just look after Nana and Granda. They've had enough to put up with.'

Then she put down her bags and held out her arms. But when he rushed into them, she was gone, and he was lying wide awake, staring up at the dark.

Somehow he knew there was something still to come.

God, the setter of mousetraps, was not mocked.

14

It was getting dark, as Sonny and Jackie Robinson came out of school. A typical early December evening, spitting on to rain, so they turned their raincoat collars up, and fled along before the wind, with the rain spots hitting on the backs of their bare knees, under their raincoats.

They parted outside the newsagent's. It was Monday night, and Sonny was picking up his *Wizard*. It suddenly came to him it was nearly a year . . .

He didn't dawdle, just shoved the *Wizard* into his pocket. Nana would be out shopping, and Granda at his ship's chandlers, where he still helped out in the afternoons in winter, when there was no gardening to be done. There would be so much to do, to make the house cosy for their coming home. The Red Duster to lower and take in, though it was long after sunset. Blackout curtains to draw, the fire to light, that Nana had left laid ready, with paper and sticks. The paraffin lamps . . .

He went through the wire, past the sentry box. There were two sentries on duty, that he knew and liked, who called him 'Sunny Jim'. One of them said, 'Hurrying home to feed that dog of yours?' Blitz was quite a favourite with all the sentries now, though he always peed on the corner of their sentry box; and also on their sandbags for good measure. They just laughed and said, 'Keeps the flies off in summer, and the Jerries in winter!'

Sonny looked ahead through the murk. There were no lights on in the Old Coastguard Station; and his guts scrunched up a bit, like they always did. A sort of fear some Jerry might have crept in silently, when their backs were turned.

'G'night, kid!'

Stiff-legged, trembling a little, he made his way to the garden gate, which swung shut with a loud click like a gunshot behind him. Blitz began to bark, a bit frantic at first, then in a more friendly way as he recognized Sonny's step. And Grimalkin was sitting calmly on the inside windowsill behind the sandbags, staring out at the dark and rain, and giving Sonny a silent miaow because he was hungry too.

So there was nobody lurking in the house . . . .

He went swiftly through his routine. Lowered the limp, wet, drooping flag, and carried it, a sodden weight, over his left hand, while he fumbled for his key with his right. He would drape the flag lovingly over a chair-back to dry, once the fire was really going.

The fire took, first match, racing up through the crumpled newspaper, making the sticks settle deeper, like a bird on its nest, licking up hungrily at the wet shiny coal. Then, draw the kitchen blackout, and light the row of lamps Nana had left ready, by the leaping glow of the fire. Already it was feeling cosy . . .

He had just lit the last lamp, and was rolling up his sleeves to tackle the bowl of potatoes Nana had left ready for peeling in an enamel basin of water, when he saw the daddy-long-legs cruising across the room. It was a huge one, a whopper. It looked nearly as big as a Jerry bomber, and he hated it nearly as much. He loved most insects, ladybirds and moths especially, but he hated the way daddy-long-legs hung about the back of your head and scraped against your bare ears with their scratchy, traily legs. Given half a chance, they got down the back of your neck . . . It was long past the season for them; but this one must have been hibernating or something, and been awakened by the sudden warmth of the fire. He backed off and grabbed an old copy of Granda's *Daily Express* and prepared to swat it.

But it had no interest in him. It made straight for the biggest and brightest oil-lamp and banged into the glass with that awful persistent pinging.

And then suddenly it went down inside, between the shade and the glass chimney. He could still hear it pinging, and see its shadow, magnified on the frosted shade. It must be getting pretty hot down there . . .

He squinted down between the shade and the hot chimney cautiously. It was hurling itself against the chimney, mad to reach the flame. Silly thing, it would do itself an injury . . . then he noticed that one of its long, crooked legs had already fallen off. As he watched, another broke off. But still the creature hurled itself against the chimney. Another leg went, then another, and there was a stink of burning that was not paraffin. Then its whole body fell against the chimney with a sharp sizzle, and lay still at last, just a little dirty mark. There was a tiny wisp of smoke.

A flamer, he thought, not like von Richthofen. And

shuddered, because it had been a living thing. Felt a bit sick and went back to the potatoes.

It was then that the siren went. He ran to the door, slipped through the blackout curtain and went to the gate to look for Nana and Granda. It was quite dark by that time; but he heard a distant fizz, and saw the first searchlight go on at the Castle. A dim, poor yellow beam at first, but quickly growing to a blinding blue-white as the arcing elements heated up. So bright it almost looked solid. High up, little wisps of cloud trailed through the beam, like cigarette smoke. Then another beam went on, and another. Four, five, six, all swinging out seawards, groping for Jerry like the fingers of a giant robot's hand. And more searchlights still; across the river at South Shields, distant around Blyth. It made him proud; we were ready for them, waiting.

But in the dim, blue, reflected light, which lit up the pier-approach road brighter than moonlight, there was no sign of Nana and Granda. He could see the two sentries at the check-point, huddled down behind their sandbags, the ends of their fags like little red pin-points. They'd be in trouble for that, if this raid was more than another false alarm. You could see a fag-end from three miles up, Granda said . . .

But otherwise, the pier-approach was empty. And there was no chance of Nana and Granda coming now; the wardens would force them down some shelter, till the raid was over. He was on his own, to look after the fortress and Blitz and Grimalkin. He felt a silly impulse to run up and join the sentries; but they'd only send him back under cover. Besides, it was time to be brave. He checked that the stirrup-pump worked, with its bucket of water. Then he did what he was supposed to do, and went down the cellar to shelter. Blitz and Grimalkin were there already.

But there was nothing to do down there, just the sacks of potatoes and swedes, and the dusty rows of elderberry wine. He should sit down on the bunk and be good. But it was horribly cold and he couldn't hear anything. For all he knew, the Jerries might be overhead now, and the house roof on fire with incendiaries, and how would he know? In an air-raid, Granda was always nipping upstairs for a look-see. As the person in charge, so should he. Or so he told himself.

He crept upstairs, leaving Blitz and Grimalkin in safety. Nothing was altered; nothing was on fire. Outside the door, everything was quiet, except for some frantic dog barking on and on, up in the town.

And then he heard it; very faint. Vroomah, vroomah, vroomah. A single plane, out over the sea. Jerry was coming. The plane got louder, and there were more, many more, behind. The sea was full of their echoes. His stomach drew itself up into a fist. Not scared, just ready.

And then the whole blue scene turned a brighter, weirder blue. High up, bunches of blinding blue stars, illuminating the huddled rooftops of the town as bright as day. The clusters of brilliant blue stars swung and swayed; travelled drifting across each other. The solitary leading Jerry was dropping flares to mark the targets, dropping the dreaded chand-eliers. Sonny felt like a poor black fly, outlined on a spotless white tablecloth. Helpless.

But others were not so helpless. The whole night scene suddenly turned from blue to bright yellow. The earth shook under his feet and the universe seemed to crack apart like an egg. The Castle guns had fired. He waited, counting under his breath. Seventeen, eighteen, nineteen. Four brilliant white stars in the sky, out to sea, burned black holes in his eyes. They were in a W-shape, and everywhere he looked now, there were four black dots in a W-shape. Then the sound of the explosions, rolling in across the water like waves. Then the echoes going away down the coast, off every cliff, fainter and fainter.

Then, out to sea still, where the bright W had been, the searchlights were clustering now. Five, then ten. Something tiny and bright, like a little minnow, was weaving and twisting, caught inside the cone of the searchlights.

They had caught the solitary dropper of chandeliers. Now, while his friends still droned in, still out of range, every gun on Tyneside seemed to be firing at the twisting minnow. Now it was falling, falling, still twisting frantically. Taking evasive action. And it suddenly succeeded. The cone of searchlights was empty. Sonny groaned aloud with frustration.

But the gunners had not missed. A little flame blossomed red in the dark sky below the searchlights. Blossomed and grew. To a bright falling comet.

A flamer! A Jerry in flames! Burn, burn! All his hate was surging through him now. He imagined the Jerries, fighting to get out, and failing. Screaming and twisting as the flames caught them.

Then the bright comet hit the sea, and went out,

and the hissing noise came across the waters of the harbour.

And suddenly, Sonny *knew*. This had been no ordinary Jerry bomber. This one had been alone, leading, marking the targets for the others. Only a pilot who knew the river and the docks would be used for that kind of job . . .

He just knew that this was the one, the Flying Pencil. Who had come once too often, been caught at last.

Mam was avenged; Dad was avenged; God was not mocked.

Now the main body of the raid was sweeping in overhead. But they hardly mattered. The guns were firing among them now, their shells bursting over the town. There was, in the air, the whisper of falling shrapnel from the guns. He ducked back into the doorway, ready to whip down the shelter. He was not such a fool as to get himself killed by falling British shrapnel, not in his moment of glory, when everything had come right. He would go down the cellar now, and cuddle Blitz, and gloat that God had cast down his Enemy, the Evil One.

He turned for a last glance.

And saw it, quite clear, in the blue glare of the searchlights and the yellow flashings of the guns. A white mushroom shape drifting down into the estuary. A Jerry parachute. He could even make out the tiny black swinging figure of the man beneath it.

It was not over, yet.

15

He whipped inside and grabbed Granda's old night-glasses, from where they hung on the back of the door. Focused frantically; the dark river, the piers, the lighthouses leaping around before his eyes like fleas. He just caught the black figure of the para-chutist as it plunged into the smooth waters of the harbour. The canopy of the parachute ghosted down gently on top, and lay flat on the water. There was no sign of life underneath it; only the widening rings of ripples on the smooth, oily water.

Perhaps he was dead before he hit the water, thought Sonny. Or wounded. Perhaps he's drowning now. He felt nothing but a fascinated coldness; like when he'd watched a spider, in Granda's shed, trap and kill a big bluebottle.

There was suddenly a hump under the parachute, as the man surfaced and struggled to free himself. Then he broke out in a flurry of foam and frantic arms and legs. Sonny could see quite clearly, through the glasses, the tight German flying-helmet that made his head look like a seal's. The RAF had quite dif-ferent sorts of helmets, more domed and bumpy . . .

So, he was alive. But the sailors on the boom-defence across the harbour mouth would have seen him. The boom-defence launch would be on its way to pick him up, any minute . . .

But nothing stirred from the boom. No sound of any chugging diesel engine. The sailors must all be watching the raid, as it roared upriver in a blizzard of gigantic fireworks, arcs of dull red tracer climbing ever so slowly up into the sky, the smaller golden balls from the pompoms.

The Jerry was free of his parachute now. He was looking around, working out which land was nearest.

And on the nearest land to him was the Old Coast-guard Station. Quite calmly, Sonny knew he would come. If he didn't drown on the way. God was setting his mousetrap . . . It all seemed inevitable now, from the beginning. A trap slowly working out.

Granda's shotgun stood in the corner handy, by the fireplace. But where were the shells? Granda always kept them hidden away. He said he didn't want any nasty accidents . . .

Hopelessly, Sonny pulled out all the kitchen drawers, but there were only knives and forks and spoons, corkscrews and funny old bits of metal from the far past with no names. Then he pulled out the drawers in the sideboard. But that was just draughts sets and dominoes and table mats. The photographs of Mam, and Dad in his uniform with his corporal's stripes, smiled at him from the sideboard top.

No good. But the Jerry mustn't have the shotgun. Sonny ran outside with it, and hid it behind the rain-water-butt. Then he remembered the bottles of petrol, with the rags in the top; the Molotov cocktails . . .

He did not quite see how they could be used. But he quickly took two, and hid them under the sink, behind Nana's waste-bucket.

The night had gone very quiet, now. Just flickers

and thuds in the distance, and the usual pink glow growing over the docks upriver. He took the night-glasses to the garden wall, and searched the waters of the harbour, and finally found a black seal-like blob, moving ahead of a dark arrowhead of ripples. He must keep the Jerry in sight, all the way. He must not lose sight of him again. It was tense and exciting, like when he was out hunting rats in the shipyard with Dad.

So he watched the Jerry wading ashore across the flat rocks, where Dad had shot the seagulls so long ago. First the shoulders, and then the bulky flying suit that made him look like a bear, a bear coming dripping out of the water. The cliff was about fifty feet high at this point; soft, brown, crumbling soil, loosened by the rain, and made slippery by the Jerry's own drippings. He heard the man swear in German, as his feet slipped away from under him, and he slid full-length back to the rocks. A giggle grew in his throat, but he pressed his lips tight closed, and no sound came out.

The German was a long time climbing the cliff; he made very heavy weather of it, grunting and gasping and swearing. But at last he levered himself on to the grass of the cliff-edge, and Sonny knew it was time to slip noiselessly back into the house.

He did consider running to warn the sentries. But they would just come and take the man away, and that would be the end of it. And somehow, he knew, that was not the end that was meant for this one . . .

He ran upstairs, and peeped out of the window of Nana's darkened bedroom, where the blackout was

150

not drawn. Watched the Jerry's shambling approach. The Jerry reached the gate and seemed to hesitate. He looked hard towards the pier-approach. But then he seemed to see the wire and the sentries, and the next moment he was moving silently up the garden path.

Sonny ran downstairs and into the kitchen, and sat in a chair by the now-blazing fire. He did not want to give Jerry a fright. Jerry might have a pistol. They said they carried pistols, just like British aircrew. Sonny had no wish to get shot by accident, before he had done what he had to do.

He heard the back door start to creak cautiously open. Again, he had the impulse to giggle. Jerry thought he was being so clever . . . Sonny picked up his copy of the *Wizard* and pretended to be deep in it.

The kitchen door swung open. Sonny looked up.

The Jerry was huge; he filled the doorway, muddy and black and shining and dripping on to Nana's lino. He trailed tentacles from his body, with little, tiny bits of shiny metal on the ends. His bright yellow life jacket was inflated, making him look even bigger. And he didn't look human, with that tight leather flying-helmet crushing his skull in, so that only his green eyes showed, and his long pale nose, and his mouth, gaping like a fish's, showing green tombstone teeth.

And in his left hand, the pistol Sonny had been expecting. A Luger automatic. He recognized it from the picture in *War Weekly*. And the cocking-handle was pulled right back, and the round black hole in the end of the barrel pointed straight at the *Wizard*, held in front of Sonny's midriff.

151

'Odders?' he shouted. 'Udders . . . odders . . . others?' He stared round him wildly, eyes wide, ears cocked.

Sonny knew what he meant. Was there anybody else in the house?

'*Nein*,' he said. That was what they said in the war comics. He felt a little glow of pride. Till the German grabbed him up roughly, and thrust him out into the hall in front of him, using him as a human shield. Shouting '*Raus, raus!*' and pushing him cruelly, when he moved too slowly.

They went through the dark empty bedrooms. Then the rooms in the watchtower. His own room, with the Jerry still dripping on a comic he'd left on the floor. Then the very top, the balcony. Outside, the gun-flashes seemed to be moving south; the rest of the Jerry bombers were going home another way. It must make Jerry feel a bit lonely. He alone was left.

Like the last Norseman must have felt, when they hunted him down, and nailed his skin to the church door, so long ago.

Now Sonny was being bundled downstairs again. He was pushed so roughly that he fell and slid down four stairs. The huge cruel hand dragged him upright, belted him one across the ear. '*Raus, raus!*'

The Jerry saw the cellar door, slightly ajar. He pushed Sonny towards it.

'Don't *push*!' shouted Sonny. 'The stairs are steep.'

He was still shoved down them. He landed on all fours at the bottom, and hurt his knees.

The Jerry glanced round, at the sacks and bottles and Granda's scythe hanging on the whitewashed wall. He was still glancing round when a small and furious bundle, barking like a fiend, hurled itself at his ankle.

The Jerry swore, struck down with the gun, making Blitz yelp. Two more savage blows, two more yelps, and then the Jerry kicked his foot and Blitz flew across the room, hit the wall with a thud, and lay silent, in a pathetically small heap.

That was the point when Sonny made up his mind the Jerry must *die*. His mind had been a bit wild and fuzzy till then, but now it was quite hard and firm and cold. It was just a matter of waiting for a chance . . .

The Jerry was staring at Grimalkin; who was glaring back, hunched on the table, ears flattened. Grimalkin spat; the Jerry raised the pistol, then appeared to change his mind, and bundled Sonny back upstairs. He sat down in a rocker in the kitchen, and seemed to relax, now he knew the house was empty. He pulled off his flying-helmet. It didn't make him look any prettier. He had blond hair, not cropped, but long and greasy as if it hadn't been washed for a month. And his green eyes were too close together. Nana always said you should never trust a man whose eyes were too close together.

The Jerry pointed the gun at Sonny and shouted, 'Fut . . . fud . . .' He pointed at his mouth, and pretended to munch his big tombstone teeth.

What could Sonny do but go to the larder? Get the half-loaf that would have to do supper and tomorrow's breakfast. The butter dish from the top shelf, with the remains of the week's ration of butter and marge, mixed up together to last longer. He began to cut a thin slice, but the Jerry pushed him aside, cut the loaf in half, smeared all the butter and marge on it, and the remains of a jar of jam that his green eyes had spotted. He put the gun down and began to tear the bread off in large chunks and stuff them in his mouth.

Sonny eyed the distance to the gun lying there. The Jerry saw him eyeing it, and moved it out of reach. When he had finished the loaf, he picked up the pistol again and went into the larder himself, groping his big hand along the shelves, picking up the cheese ration, and a couple of half-stale cakes, and stuffing them into his mouth in turn. He was gulping stuff so quickly you could tell it hurt him to swallow. But he still went on doing it. He swallowed three slightly shrivelled apples, then came across a full jar of jam and began eating it with a spoon, direct from the jar. Didn't they feed them, before they went on a raid? Were the Jerries *really* starving, as the Ministry of Information used to say in the Phoney War?

Having emptied the larder, the Jerry returned to his rocking-chair. He seemed a bit calmer; he belched loudly, then grinned, trying to make a joke of it, wanting Sonny to laugh.

Sonny kept his face absolutely straight. Waiting his chance.

And when it came, it was so simple. Like a gift from the Gods.

'*Trinken*,' said the Jerry. '*Trink* . . . drink!'

Sonny kept his face straight, sullen, though his heart leapt. He made an empty gesture towards the teapot . . .

'*Nein, nein!* roared the Jerry. '*Trink!*' He mimed

the gesture of taking a cork out of a bottle; lifting the invisible bottle to his lips.

Sonny raised his eyebrows and pointed down towards the cellar. The Jerry nodded; he had seen the bottles of Nana's elderberry on the shelf down there. He lumbered to his feet and came as far as the cellar door and watched Sonny descend.

Sonny went to Blitz first. The little dog still lay where he had fallen. In the light from the paraffin lamp, Sonny could not be sure if he was still breathing or not. He felt him; he felt warmish and floppy, but Sonny knew that didn't mean anything. It took time for things to go cold and stiff, Granda said.

With tears of rage in his eyes, Sonny turned to the bottles on the shelf. There was this year's stuff, still fermenting, harmless. There was 1939, 1938, the last happy years of peace.

And there was 1937; the lethal stuff that a year ago had done such harm to the curate. It would be even stronger now. He lifted down three bottles of the 1937, and cradled them so gently in his arms as he climbed the stairs.

'*Gut*,' grunted the German. '*Gut*. Goo-od.' He made a corkscrew gesture with his free hand.

Silent and correct as a butler in a movie, Sonny fetched him the corkscrew.

The Jerry had trouble with the corkscrew; his hands were shaking. Suddenly, in a rage, he smashed the neck of the bottle against the brick surround of the range; the neck broke off, and tinkled among the ashes. Then the Jerry threw back his head, and opened his tombstone mouth, and poured half the bottle down his throat. Sonny eased himself contentedly into a chair; now it was only a matter of waiting. He thought about the petrol bombs, the Molotov cocktails under the sink, and his stomach crawled with excitement.

The Jerry stared at the half-empty bottle. He was baffled. Elderberry tasted so fresh and harmless; the look on the Jerry's face was the same one Granda had when he said,

'Gnat's pee!'

Still, the Jerry must have been quite thirsty. He finished the bottle in three more gulps.

Helpfully, Sonny reached for the corkscrew and began to open a second bottle.

The Jerry smiled. '*Ja. Wein. Gut.*' He took the second bottle from Sonny's offering hand. He stretched out his wet legs to the blaze, and let the gun droop over the arm of the rocker. Then he had a long think, mouthing words to himself, and finally said, slowly but quite clearly, '*Englander* . . . are not . . . our natural enemy!' He seemed very pleased with this, took another swig and announced, '*Englander* . . . little bruder . . . brothers.' He had a lot of bother with the word 'brother'. Then he put down the bottle for a minute, and reached across and patted Sonny on the knee. Then he picked up the bottle again, and offered it to Sonny, indicating that he drink too.

'Drink, little brother.'

Sonny made a mess of it. He didn't want to drink, and yet he knew he had to. Or the Jerry might suspect an attempt to poison him. So Sonny drank, and it went down the wrong way, and he sprayed it all over the place, and went into an agonising fit of coughing.

The Jerry threw up his head and laughed as if he thought this was hilarious. He got up and banged Sonny on the back painfully. Sonny's back crept in disgust, at the touch of that hand.

'*Wein* . . . not for . . . little brother!' Oh, he thought it *such* a joke.

Then he sat down again, and said, solemn as an owl, '*Englander*, little brother . . . but Europe corrupt . . . we must make a New Order. Then . . . all happy!'

Sonny just waited. The elderberry was starting to have its deadly effect. The Jerry was slumping lower in his chair. His strange speech was starting to slur, as if his tongue and lips were getting too much to manage. And the hand that held the gun was playing with it, feverishly. Sonny grew afraid it might go off.

And then the Jerry wasn't grinning any more. He looked at Sonny like a blinking owl and said, 'Drink toast to Rudi . . . *mein Kamerad.*' Then he said, '*Rudi ist tot* . . . dead.' He blinked again, and Sonny realized suddenly he was blinking back tears. '*Und Heini ist tot. Und Maxi und Karl. Alle . . . tot.*' The tears began to stream silently down his face. '*Meine Kameraden.*' He drank heavily from the second bottle. Then he began to sing, in a maudlin dreadful voice, that cracked and broke on every phrase. Something about '*Ich hatt einen Kameraden*'. And Sonny knew he was singing about the crew of his plane.

And his heart might have softened. Until he thought of Mam and Dad and Blitz, and the God who is not mocked.

Then he just went on waiting.

Finally, the Jerry stopped. An alarmed look grew

157

on his face. He tried to get up, and failed, the rocker swinging and slewing under him, so he fell heavily back into it. He tried again, pressing down with both hands on the chair-arms. And since he had a bottle in one hand, and the gun in the other, he didn't make it again. The hand that held the bottle opened and the bottle fell on to Nana's clippie rug with a dull clunk, and rolled towards Sonny, spilling out a trail of elderberry that stained as dark as blood.

Slowly, on the third attempt, the Jerry managed to lever himself to his feet. He stared at Sonny, his face with its gaping tombstone mouth unreadable. Sonny wondered whether he was going to be shot. Whether, in an instant, there would be a bang and an agony, then darkness and he would wake up with Mam and Dad . . .

But perhaps the Jerry remembered sending for the wine himself; sending his little slave labourer.

Instead, the Jerry made a wavering track for the door, crashing into the furniture in his way, hurting himself badly, and gasping with the pain. He reminded Sonny of something . . .

The daddy-long-legs, in the oil lamp. Like it, he had come flying in; like it, he was dashing himself to pieces. Sonny almost laughed out loud. Except that pistol was wavering all over the room . . .

Then it went off. The noise was deafening. A panel of the kitchen door suddenly ceased to exist, and splinters flew everywhere, and there was that Guy Fawkes smell, and the resinous piney smell of splintered wood.

Then the gun went off again, and the Jerry cried out. And Sonny saw blood welling from the leg of

158

his wet flying suit. Dark red, flowing, glistening. And then, with a wild yell, he was gone out of the back door, and the wind was blowing in.

Sonny ran to the door, slipped through the blackout curtain, his hand automatically rearranging it behind him. He peered right.

Against the pink glow that was Newcastle burning, he saw the Jerry lurching like a Saturday-night drunk among the ragged Brussels sprouts of Granda's garden.

He was heading for . . . the early potato patch. From which, so long ago, he and Granda had taken the soil for the sandbags. With the coming of winter, it had filled up with water. They called it the duck-pond now. Granda had even spoken of getting a few Khaki Campbells or Aylesburys, for the eggs . . .

With a sudden coldness inside him, Sonny suddenly knew he wasn't going to need the Molotov cocktails. God's little mousetrap was going to work without him doing anything. He only had to watch, as he had once watched the spider catch the bluebottle. God would do the rest. God was not mocked.

The Jerry, as if fated, drew nearer and nearer the edge of the hole. Once, he veered away towards safety; but as if something drew him to his fate, he wavered back. There was a gasp, a slip, a cry in German, then a splash, a huge splash. He was in. Headfirst. His gun wouldn't do him any good now, down in the water.

There were more gasps. What sounded like a cry for help.

Sonny crept closer, to watch.

A hand came in sight, above the edge of the hole. A

159

hand grasping at the smooth, muddy, squelchy sides, and getting no grip and falling back again. Again, the hand appeared, and then fell back.

It did not come a third time.

Sonny crept up, and looked over the edge.

Four feet down, the water glinted; and in the water, only a series of dark humps. As he watched, a burst of greasy, muddy bubbles broke the surface, from the smallest, furthest-away bump.

Just a little more waiting, and it would be over.

It was then that Sonny thought of Granda's garden; and the Old Coastguard House. Where Mam had been happy; where Mam, he was sure, still came. Where Dad might still come, in dreams.

But if the Jerry died, *he* would be in the garden. Always. You would not be able to go in the garden without looking at that patch of soil, and remembering.

He would poison the whole garden. Then there would never be happiness again. He might come in dreams, huge, dripping, muddy, trailing wires, faceless like a seal under his flying-helmet. He would make sleep unthinkable.

More bubbles broke the surface of the muddy water. Perhaps there was still time to cleanse the garden.

Sonny didn't hesitate. He leapt down into the hole, trampling on the squidgy mass that was the dying Jerry. Jerry raised his head and groaned, a dreadful noise. Sonny knelt and reached for his head, and held it above the water. But it was heavy, so heavy. Jerry wriggled, and Sonny's hand slipped, and the head

160

went down into the black water again, and there were more bubbles.

Then he saw what he must do. Raise Jerry's head, and get his own legs under it.

It was a struggle, but at last, groaning and panting to himself, he managed it. And sat with his back braced against the side of the hole, with the freezing water creeping up to his waist, then his chest, and his own bottom squidging lower and lower into the mud, every time he tried to ease himself, under the enormous weight.

And so he sat, as the last raid droned in overhead, and the guns lit up the sky, and the searchlights searched in vain, and the shrapnel came whispering down, and even thudded once among the very Brussels sprouts behind his head. Sat, with only a faint sound of barking from the Old Coastguard Station cellar to comfort him. At least Blitz was alive, after all. There would be no more death.

And it was there, after the all-clear had gone, that Granda found him, coming in response to his faint calls, after Sonny had heard the garden gate click.

'God love the bairn!' cried Granda. 'What's this?'

'A Jerry,' gasped Sonny.

'Can ye hang on a bit?' yelled Granda. 'Aah'll fetch the sentries.'

Granda knew what he was talking about. It took the three of them to get the Jerry out, and they had to summon an ambulance to take him away under guard to Preston Hospital. He had come round by then. From the stretcher, his huge hand grabbed Sonny's.

'*Kamerad*,' he gasped. '*Freund*!'

Sonny's face went stony, though he could not get his hand free.

'Dornier?' he asked at last, coldly. 'Dornier?'

The pilot's muddy face was a picture of bewilderment.

'Nein,' he said, puzzled. 'Nein. Heinkel! Heinkel!'

Then they took him away.

Granda looked at the hole. 'By,' he said, 'Aah often went fishin' as a lad, but Aah never cowt anything as big as that. Aah'll have to get that hole filled in. *Anybody* could drown in it.'

'Yes,' said Sonny, flatly. He felt so weary he could hardly stand.

They went into the kitchen. Granda looked at the shattered kitchen door, the bottle on the hearth rug, the blood on the doormat, then he noticed the two Molotov cocktails under the sink. His grey eyebrows went up, nearly vanishing under his grey hair.

'By, Aah can tell there's a tale to tell here! An' look at that dog, hoppin' around on three legs . . .'

'Yes,' said Sonny flatly.

'But here's yer nana comin' up the path. By God, there'll be hell to pay when she sees that door.' He picked up the bottle off the hearth rug. 'We'd better get tidied up, an' save the tale till later, eh?'

And that was where they left it.

Also by Robert Westall

The Machine Gunners

'Some bright kid's got a gun and 2000 rounds of
live ammo. And that gun's no peashooter. It'll go
through a brick wall at a quarter of a mile.'

Chas McGill has the second-best collection of war
souvenirs in Garmouth, and he desperately wants
it to be the best. When he stumbles across the
remains of a German bomber crashed in the woods
– its shiny, black machine-gun still intact – he grabs
his chance. Soon he's masterminding his own war
effort, with dangerous and unexpected results . . .

'Not just the best book so far written for children
about the Second World War, but also a metaphor
for now.'
Times Literary Supplement

'No better junior novel than this has appeared for a
long time . . . Indeed, adult readers would learn
a great deal from it.'
The School Librarian

WINNER OF THE CARNEGIE MEDAL

Fathom Five

The sequel to *The Machine Gunners*

The current grew stronger. It was drawing the raft towards the back of the towering ship, faster and faster.

'The propellers!' screamed Chas. 'They're sucking us in!'

Chas McGill has set out to prove that there really is a German spy in wartime Garmouth, sending information to enemy U-Boats. But what started as a bet with his best friend Cem soon goes far beyond a game. And Chas's obsessive search for the elusive spy leads him to the most terrible decision of his life.

'A writer of rare talent.'
Michael Morpurgo

Blitzcat

She made her way down the cliff, and on to the beach. At the edge of the waves, she stopped, shaking her wet paws. She knew that somewhere ahead was her person, but far, far away. She miaowed plaintively; stood staring at the moving blur of uncrossable sea.

She led the way to safety, out of the blazing hell of blitzed Coventry. People touched her for luck; feared her as an omen of disaster. Wherever she went, she changed lives . . .

From her beginning to her end she never wavered.

She was the Blitzcat.

'Westall's writing has always been strong and vivid but he has rarely written as confidently as this'
Times Literary Supplement

Robert Westall titles
available from Macmillan Children's Books

ROBERT WESTALL

Blitzcat	0 330 39861 X	£5.99
Fathom Five	0 330 39862 8	£4.99
The Machine Gunners	0 330 33428 X	£4.99
A Time of Fire	0 330 39864 4	£4.99
Ghosts and Journeys	0 330 30904 8	£3.99
The Wind Eye	0 330 32234 6	£3.99
Stormsearch	0 330 48270 X	£4.99